THE MYSTERIOUS LADY
OF
LAKEVIEW

THE MYSTERIOUS LADY
OF
LAKEVIEW

Judy Conlin

iUniverse, Inc.
New York   Bloomington

THE MYSTERIOUS LADY OF LAKEVIEW

This is a work of fiction. All of the characters, names, incidents, organizations, and dialogue in this novel are either the products of the author's imagination or are used fictitiously.

iUniverse books may be ordered through booksellers or by contacting:

iUniverse
1663 Liberty Drive
Bloomington, IN 47403
www. iuniverse. com
1-800-Authors (1-800-288-4677)

Because of the dynamic nature of the Internet, any Web addresses or links contained in this book may have changed since publication and may no longer be valid. The views expressed in this work are solely those of the author and do not necessarily reflect the views of the publisher, and the publisher hereby disclaims any responsibility for them.

ISBN: 978-1-4401-7373-8 (sc)
ISBN: 978-1-4401-7372-1 (ebook)
ISBN: 978-1-4401-7371-4 (hc)

Printed in the United States of America

iUniverse rev. date: 9/29/2009

Acknowledgments

It takes a great many people to bring a book to fruition. Although there is no way I could possibly acknowledge the many people who helped make this book possible, I would like to mention some of the main ones.

Thank you to:

The Havana Public Library, who allowed me to work on my laptop in their building on those days when I just had to get out of the house. I completed a great amount of research within their walls.

The Friends of the Gadsden County Library, who buy my books for the libraries in their system, who continue to support my endeavors, and who featured me as keynote speaker at their Author's Luncheon.

The Havana Book Club, who deserve mention because of their continued support and encouragement.

The Tallahassee Democrat and The Leon County Library for publicizing my efforts.

The bookstores, associations, and downtown merchants who arrange book-signing events for my books.

Wendy Rabe, former newspaper editor, for lending her expertise in proofing and editing this work. Her many suggestions contributed greatly to improving this book.

The Havana Herald and The Wakulla News for not only running my weekly columns, but for promoting my complete and "in the works" books.

For all my readers out there who provide much-appreciated feedback.

LEE AND CORRAL FAMILY TREES

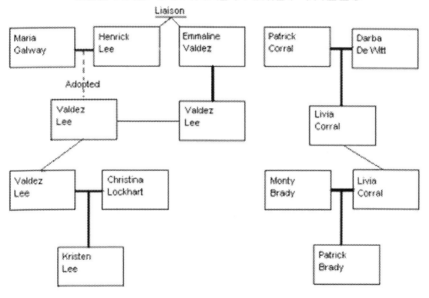

CHAPTER ONE

"Miss Lee, will you check my finger wave?"

"What colors should I mix for Spun Gold, Miss Lee?"

"Where's the key for the dispensary, Miss Lee?"

Kristen stood in the center of the cosmetology lab wishing (not for the first time) that she'd inherited a surname other than the one her budding cosmetologists repeated at least five hundred times a day.

"Miss Lee, Miss Lee, Miss Lee," she murmured as she attempted to meet the needs of those students nearest her. "I wish my name were Mehitabel."

"Miss Mehitabel, Miss Mehitabel," grinned Linda Larkin, waving a mannequin head under her nose. "Is this worth an A?"

"B," Kristen grinned back. She caught a glimpse of herself in the mirror of one of the workstations scattered throughout the room. Running her fingers through her short, red hair and gazing at her freckled face, she could understand why the principal often couldn't tell her from one of her high school students. She had unruly red curls, a round freckled face, and, despite her twenty-six years, she stood only five feet tall. She tried to disguise her youthful appearance with three-inch heels, vertical stripes, and her impression of a Mona Lisa smile—but by quarter of three on a Friday afternoon, the smile had long been discarded.

"Time to clean up," she announced, as she delivered the required key to a pert little blonde named Suzie.

The students milled around apathetically, anxious to leave, and hoping the bell would ring before they completed sweeping up shorn locks, putting away supplies, and finishing the other cleaning chores that were part of their daily routine. Kristen sighed. God, she hated Friday afternoons. "No one's leaving until this place is ship-shape, so hop to it," she said firmly.

The students put a little more energy into their half-hearted efforts, giving her weak grins completely lacking in malice. It was a game to them, a game they never tired of playing, a sort of "nothing ventured, nothing gained" amusement.

When the room bore a reasonable resemblance to orderliness, she had the students sit down, gave them their assignments, and then dismissed them on the bell.

"Bye. Have a nice weekend."

"Bye. Don't forget to study."

"Bye. See ya Monday."

One by one, they passed by on their way out the door, the passage of each one meaning she was that much closer to beginning her own weekend. If only she wasn't so tired!

She busied herself cleaning off her desk. For once, she was going to get out at a reasonable hour. Books were thrust into the bookcase and papers were shuffled and stacked neatly, but in no particular order—so, come Monday, the reshuffling would start again.

"Hey Teach, ready to go?" It was Maggie, nursing instructor and loyal friend, who usually walked to the parking lot with her.

" No, but I'm leaving anyhow," Kristen said, stuffing her battered briefcase with her fat grade book, its papers popping out at all angles as though trying to escape the inevitable attacks of her red grading pencil. "Boy, I wish all those folks who think teachers have such a cushy job—'all those summers and vacations off'—could see what we drag home every night, and all the hours we put in on our own time just to try and keep up."

"Know what you mean," the sleek blonde nurse said, swinging her own leather case, which though also well-filled, was as shiny and unblemished as the day she had bought it. But then, that was Maggie. Kristen couldn't imagine her with a zit, with a wrinkle in her skirt, or even with a broken nail. Maggie could go through a hurricane and still be perfectly coifed, dressed, and poised. Yet, she was one of the most down-to-earth, hardworking people at the school.

Kristen locked her classroom, and the two headed out to the parking lot. "Did you put in for a leave?" Maggie asked, as soon as the room was secured. That was another of Maggie's qualities—directness.

Kristen smiled. "Yes," she said, "and the board meets tonight. Don't know what the chances of it going through are though."

"I sure hope it does. You owe it to yourself to make that trip. Just think, you may be an heiress."

"I doubt that. I think Grandfather's just curious. After all, he never saw my father after my father married my mother. Now he's old and Daddy's dead, so he needs an excuse to see his only granddaughter. Offering the possibility of an inheritance is his bait."

"How does your mother feel about you going?"

"She's all for it." Kristen grimaced. "My first impulse was to tell that old man to take a flying leap, but Mother kept saying I owed it to Daddy—that it's what Daddy would have wanted. I'm not sure that's true, but it was so good to see her taking an interest in something besides father's grave that I agreed to go if I could get the time off school."

"Well, I think it's exciting," Maggie said, putting her lithe little body behind the wheel of her sports car, a car as sleek and sophisticated as Maggie herself. Kristen raised her hand self-consciously to smooth her unruly curls, feeling frumpish before this paragon, as Maggie blithely continued. "My friend, the Mistress of Lakeview Manor. That is exciting. Just what lake does that manor view up north in New York State?"

"Lake Ontario, I think, and from what I hear, February is not the best time to be leaving Florida for that part of the country—lots of snow, wind, ice, and more snow. Sounds awful to a hothouse flower like me."

"Just why have you been summoned now? Why not this summer after school is out?"

"Ostensibly, because Grandfather isn't well. That's what the letter says, but I have a feeling it's just another manifestation of his perverse nature. After all, a man who would disown his only son because he married a dancer, a daughter of "poor white trash," is not the man I'd most like to find myself related to." Kristen shrugged, hoping to minimize her own bitterness.

"We all have relatives we don't like," Maggie said, turning the key in the ignition, "but we get to choose our friends. Call you tonight, friend, after the board meeting." Driving off, she blew Kristen a kiss.

Kristen turned to her own beat-up car. She'd had a better one, but after her father's death, she'd sold it to hire a live-in companion for her mother. This kept her needy mother on an even keel and allowed Kristen to continue to work. Her father had had a good job at Pratt and Whitney, but he and her mother had lived well beyond their means, like two happy children without a thought to the future. Kristen often felt more the parent than the child. When her father died suddenly of a heart attack, she was appalled to discover that due to his earlier pattern of drifting from job to job, and company to company, there was no widow's pension, and very little insurance money. Still, there was enough to bury him and Social Security would keep her mother cared for if she lived modestly. If Kristen got the leave, her half-salary would pay for the companion's salary, leaving precious little for necessities for herself. Still, she hoped it would go through. She was so very tired—tired of hassling the students everyday to improve their skills, tired of trying to keep up with endless paperwork, tired of preparing for clinic, competitions, open houses, mall shows, and advisory council meetings and dinners, and tired of being the strong person in the classroom and then going home and having to be strong there, too. Yes, she was tired, and they said a change is as good as rest. She hoped she would get that leave.

She smiled as she pumped the accelerator and waited for the motor to catch. Things could only get better. The smile was replaced by a look of resignation. Of course, things weren't going to get better. Of course, this old heap wasn't going to start tonight when she couldn't wait to get home. Of course, this was Friday when the building had emptied faster than a theater after someone yelled, "fire." Of course, no one was there to help her. Slowly, she retraced her steps back into the school. God, she was tired.

CHAPTER TWO

▼

Two weeks later Kristen smiled, holding her breath as she pumped the accelerator and waited for the engine to catch. This time it purred into life as gently as a kitten. "Jake sure did a job on this car," she said to her friend, remembering when she'd been stuck at the school. At seven o'clock that evening, the adult auto mechanic's class was scheduled and the amiable instructor had taken Kristen under his wing and her car into his shop. By the time the car was functional, the board meeting was over and Kristen had found out she'd gotten her leave.

"It was probably a labor of love after one look from those deep green eyes of yours," Maggie giggled, as Kristen drove back onto the New York State Thruway leaving the rest stop where they'd just finished a cup of coffee. Kristen still couldn't believe Maggie was with her. She had declared she was riding to Buffalo, New York, with Kristen and then taking a plane back south. After all, she had said, she had a four-day weekend for Patriot's Day, she'd always wanted to see snow, and what cheaper way to go than to hitch a ride with Kristen. Besides, they might get snowed in. Buffalo was always getting snowed in.

Kristen wasn't fooled. Beautiful Maggie had hundreds of things to do with a four-day weekend that were much more interesting than spending it on the road. It was a measure of her generosity and friendship that she'd chosen to accompany Kristen. They'd taken turns driving and sleeping and made much better time than Kristen ever could have alone. They hadn't run into snow until Pennsylvania. Then, for two girls unused to the white powder, there were some pretty scary scenarios on the winding hilly roads. By contrast, the New York State Thruway, while slick and slippery, was mainly clear of snow.

"The next exit must be ours. It says Transit Road." Kristen smiled at Maggie. "Are you sure you want to stay at the Airport Sheraton tonight? You could continue on with me to Grandfather's and I could bring you back to catch your plane tomorrow."

"Absolutely not. If you think I want to butt in on that meeting, you've got to be kidding. We'll have a nice dinner, then I'll settle down in my nice quiet, warm room, and you can face the ogre on your own." She yawned. "Snow isn't all it's cracked up to be. It looks so soft and fluffy in pictures, but I never realized it was so cold. It would be a lot more fun if it was warm and comfy, like the white sand on our Florida beaches."

Kristen's breath caught in her throat. "I'm going to miss you, Maggie. No one could be a better friend."

Maggie ran a hand over her smooth pageboy. "Just find a nice place for dinner," she said. "I'd like to look some of the Northern men over before I head south again."

They found a nice place for dinner at the lively restaurant in the airport hotel, and if the many admiring glances that came Maggie's way were any indication, she would have the opportunity to look over many Northern men if she so desired. Kristen, in her simple slacks and shirt, might have felt outclassed if she'd been with anyone else, but part of Maggie's charm was her unique ability to minimize her own importance and maximize that of her friends. Oh yes, Kristen was going to miss her. She glanced at her watch. "Six o'clock," she said. "I guess I should get going. Lakeview is only about forty-five minutes north of here, but it's dark and the roads could be bad, so I'd better go." She really didn't want to leave.

The two girls embraced and Maggie thrust a rectangular package into Kristen's hand. "Don't open this now, but if you get stranded between here and your grandfather's in that old wreck of yours, you can take a peek. In fact, I insist upon it. Do I have your solemn promise?"

Kristen nodded, putting the parcel into the glove box to cover the lump in her throat that made it hard to swallow

Maggie, poised as ever, waved airily and disappeared into the comfort of her bright warm hotel, while Kristen drove off into the bleak, cold darkness. All the cheeriness in her life seemed to have gone with Maggie, leaving harsh reality in its place. She felt like turning back and joining her friend, but stubbornness was too much a part of her character. Deliberately, she stuck out her tongue at life in general and began singing, "*Over the river and through the woods, to Grandfather's house I go,"* at the top of her lungs. It was amazing how much better she felt.

She turned left on Transit Road and continued north through a well-lit busy commercial area, a tiny community called Swarmsville, the larger city of Lockport, and on into the night, which now, if possible, seemed darker and lonelier than before. Snow had drifted in spots and traffic was sparse on the small side roads that her maps told her led to her grandfather's home. As more flurries began, Kristen, in her white car in this empty white world, had an eerie feeling of non-existence.

CHAPTER THREE

▼

Kristen gazed at the house, a sprawling iceberg floating in a sea of white, while little shivers ran down her spine—shivers that she knew weren't just from the austere weather. Why had she come here anyhow? A grandfather who couldn't forgive his own son must be as cold and dreary as the night. She longed for the reassuring presence of Maggie.

The windows softened the house's stern expression. They were long. Kristen figured they must reach from floor to ceiling. A few were spilling over with warm yellow light which fanned out making golden arches on the snow beneath them. The rest remained dark and unwelcoming. A widow's walk at the top of the house created a somber picture.

Kristen made her way through drifts of whipped cream—which felt more like ice cream—to the back of the house. She wasn't sure why she had chosen this course since the welcoming light spilled out only from the front. Perhaps it was the feeling that she really wasn't welcome. She found a back door, and with a hand that trembled from cold, nerves, or both, she rapped sharply on the stout door. When no one appeared, she berated herself for her shortsightedness and gazed unenthusiastically at the long unshoveled path back around the house. Hunching her shoulders against the wind now swirling around her, she was contemplating the best route to another entrance when the door silently opened.

Kristen could make out little in the dark interior, but she had the impression that a rather large female figure stood there. "I'm Kristen Lee, and I'm here to visit my grandfather," she said timidly.

"Yes, we've been expecting you. Please come in." The voice was deep but definitely female. "I'm Hilda, Mr. Lee's nurse. The housekeeper has taken the day off to visit her daughter—an unheard-of thing around here—I mean unheard of for her to ever leave the place. Bless my soul, I don't know how the woman does it."

All the while she talked, the nurse was leading Kristen through what appeared to be a huge pantry toward a dim light. "Not that I don't like it here. I do. It's just that, set out here in the middle of nowhere with no one to talk to—well, I guess it seems a little creepy at times. I usually go on home once I get Mr. Lee tucked in for the night, but I'm staying over tonight to give Mrs. Phipps a little respite. With this storm, I'm betting she wishes she'd picked another night off."

She led Kristen into the lighted room, a huge, friendly, old-fashioned kitchen complete with fireplace. Here Kristen got her first look at Hilda. She was large—large and rectangular. Dressed all in white, she resembled nothing so much as a refrigerator—a refrigerator with appendages. She had a big smile, warm understanding eyes, and hands that looked both capable and gentle. Her persona exuded comfort and, despite the complete dissimilarity in physical appearance, she reminded Kristen of Maggie. *It must be a universal trait of nurses*, she thought to herself, *to always leave others in a much happier frame of mind.*

"I'll take you right along up to your room, if you don't mind using the back stairs," Hilda said, as Kristen hoisted her snow-covered luggage, which had been advertised as "the largest thing on wheels other than a van." The stairs were steep, and Kristen was advancing clumsily until Hilda's well-muscled right arm reached back and plucked the suitcase from her grasp as if it were a feather pillow. She led Kristen down a corridor into a beautiful rose-wallpapered room, reminiscent of an earlier era. A huge four-poster bed with a white spread and canopy dominated the space between two of the floor-to-ceiling windows that Kristen had noted earlier. Hilda hoisted the valise effortlessly onto a chest, then folded back the top linen on the bed, saying, "Bet you'd like nothing so much as a nice warm bath and a bite to eat in your room before you turn in."

Kristen stood silently as she envisioned this Amazon deftly administering a bed bath and spooning porridge into her perfectly capable self. Thankfully, the illusion vanished as Hilda showed her the doorway into the bathroom and prepared to withdraw, with the promise that she'd return with a light tray in forty-five minutes. She calculated that this would give Kristen time to unpack, take a leisurely bubble bath, and, perhaps, get a little acquainted with her immediate environment.

Kristen quickly realized that the comforting appearance of the house was somewhat deceptive. With her outdoor wear removed, she could feel a cold draft coming from the hall on one side and from the windows on the other. The plush ruby red carpet looked warm and cozy, but felt cold to her already chilled feet as she crossed it to pull the matching velvet draperies closed. This tactic helped, but when the wind howled outside, the draperies undulated as if they had a life of their own. Shivering, Kristen looked longingly at the pristine fireplace. Did it no longer work? She removed a new fleecy green robe and shaggy slippers from her luggage, along with the case containing her toiletries, and opened the door that Hilda had pointed out as leading to the bathroom.

She stood in the doorway stunned, for she was looking into a bathroom from another era. It had to be at least one hundred years old. A tin bathtub was enclosed in exquisite oak paneling. As she made her way to the old-fashioned sink, an eerie feeling came over her. She gazed into the wavy mirror above the sink, and then crumpled softly to the floor.

CHAPTER FOUR

▼

"I knew it—I just knew it. You, young lady, are just plain tuckered out. Now lean on me and I'm going to help you into your room and into your bed, and you're going to get some hot vittles into your chilled tummy."

Kristen struggled under Hilda's strong grasp. "I ... I'm sorry," she stammered.

"Tut, tut, nothing to be sorry for. I'm the one who should be sorry, sorry I didn't insist on tucking you in immediately, and sorry I left you alone up here, weak, tired, and cold as you were."

All the while, Hilda was maneuvering Kristen back into the bedroom and up the steps onto the edge of the bed, where she unobtrusively checked Kristen's pulse. "Does your head hurt?" she asked, as Kristen raised her hand to her head.

"N ... no. Nothing hurts, but do you have a hand mirror?"

Although she looked puzzled, Hilda obediently went to the dresser and picked up a gilt hand mirror. Kristen took it with a trembling hand. She scrutinized her face carefully and touched her hair on both sides. Then she simultaneously gave Hilda the mirror and a tremulous smile. "I'm okay," she said. "I'm okay now."

"Slip into your night clothes," Hilda commanded, as she tactfully turned her back. Kristen dutifully obeyed and was soon propped up in bed, sipping a delightful chicken soup and munching on a pita pocket sandwich, despite the fact that she'd eaten dinner only a short time before. *This was an odd household*, she thought to herself, *quiet as a tomb at this hour, even though they had been expecting her.* Hilda kept up a running conversation and a not-too-subtle clinical observation.

Before taking the tray, she checked Kristen's pulse once again, then admonished, "Now, you snuggle down and get a good night's sleep. In the morning, I'll bring your breakfast, so don't be getting up and about before I get here. I don't want any more accidents—not while I'm on duty."

Kristen tried to protest, for she was immensely embarrassed by the whole incident, but Hilda was adamant. Once the lights were out and the nurse's heavy footsteps disappeared far below, Kristen forced herself to count to one hundred before she turned on the bedside lamp and gazed into the gilt mirror once again. She touched her face and hair reassuringly, then turned off the light and fell quickly asleep.

Despite the heavy drapes and the lack of morning sun, Kristen's inner clock seemed to be functioning, for she woke at eight o'clock in the morning—a reasonable hour after the exhausting previous day. As she was getting her bearings, the white refrigerator peeked in, and then entered with a breakfast tray. "Thought you might as well have breakfast in bed," she said, plopping it down with competent hands.

As Kristen began to murmur in protest, Hilda interrupted.

"Nonsense. Had to fix something for my patient. Two was just as easy. When Mrs. Phipps gets back (she's due anytime now), she'll shoo me out of the kitchen, so let me enjoy my privileges while I can. Your grandfather wants to see you at ten o'clock, so eat, get dressed, poke around, and we'll meet you in the sitting room. It's at the bottom of the front stairs to the right. I must say, you're much less peaked today." With that assessment, she withdrew.

"Wait, wait a minute," Kristen called urgently. "Is there any other bathroom?"

Hilda looked puzzled. "Just one downstairs," she said, "but no one else will be using this one—it's all yours. Mr. Lee doesn't come up here anymore." She disappeared from view and Kristen could hear her sturdy legs stumping down the stairs.

She ate the granola and yogurt hungrily, but only sipped the strong "no-nonsense" coffee, trying to make it last. She wanted to put off visiting that bathroom for as long as possible and her reluctance had nothing to do with any fear of being interrupted, as Hilda had assumed.

The coffee could only last so long, however, so she finally pushed aside the tray and slid out of bed. She shivered and wrapped her robe snugly around her. *My, it was cold.* She gathered up a change of clothes and her traveling kit containing all the necessary soaps, creams, shampoos, conditioners, and cosmetics necessary to maintain that "natural" look. *Being a cosmetologist was a great help in carrying out this innocent deception,* she thought to herself.

She hesitated a moment but did not head for the bathroom. Instead, she set off to explore. She peeked into several bedrooms, all containing four-posters, chamber pots, washstands, and fireplaces (none of which were shedding any warmth this morning). She discovered a laundry area, complete with modern washer and dryer that appeared out of place, but very practical, in this old homestead. *How strange to have the washer and dryer upstairs*, she thought, *but then again, that's where most of the soiled linen and clothing would have been when the house was full.* Now, with her grandfather and the housekeeper ensconced downstairs, it must be quite a chore dragging everything up and down the long steep staircase from the kitchen that she had wearily climbed last night.

She noted there was another staircase, this one, beautiful and gracefully curved downward—presumably the front stairs that Hilda had referenced. What interested her more, however, was another set of steps extending upward. Since it was only a two-story house, she wondered where they led. Being Kristen, she decided to find out. Up she went. *The cupola, of course.* She looked around the square, unfurnished space entirely enclosed in glass. The air was absolutely frigid up here, but the view was spectacular. Completely surrounding the enclosure was a walkway with a low railing. Kristen wondered who would have enough nerve to walk around there. Off in the distance, she could see the shimmering blue of Lake Ontario. As she stared at it, an ancient sailing vessel laden with casks appeared and just as suddenly disappeared. Kristen blinked her eyes and searched the horizon. *Had there been a sailing vessel or not? Was it just an illusion? Certainly nothing was there now. No ship could have vanished so completely so quickly. It must have been an imaginative interpretation of the morning sun reflecting on snow, ice, and water.* Shaking her head, she slowly backed down the stairs and proceeded to the bathroom. Taking a deep breath, she pushed at the door.

CHAPTER FIVE

▼

As Kristen fearfully opened the bathroom door a crack, she peered in and saw the same tin bathtub she had seen the night before. Her heart was beating rapidly, with such force she was sure her robe was moving up and down. She tried to pull herself together. What in the world was the matter with her? She had never been timid; she was assertive, determined (sometimes characterized as stubborn), and very sure of herself. Her red hair went with her temper, which was usually kept under control but once aroused could be quite intense. Her strength drew weak men, but she was never attracted to them. If she was so strong, why was she acting so silly? Was it because she had been overtired last night that she allowed her imagination to get out of control? Resolutely, she opened the door wide and stepped inside.

She walked to the antique basin and filled it with water. She must prepare to meet her grandfather, a meeting that she really wasn't looking forward to. Avoiding looking into the mirror above the sink, she finished washing and brushed her teeth. With her back to the sink, she quickly dressed. Now it was time for hair and makeup. However, this meant she must face the mirror. Deliberately, she turned and gazed into the glass. All she saw was a determined Kristen, with squared jaw and wide eyes looking back. She breathed a sigh of relief at her foolishness and quickly tamed her short, unruly locks into some semblance of order and dabbed on makeup. She gazed at her reflection, wishing she didn't always look so wholesome. Suddenly, a slight dizziness overtook her. She stared into the mirror. The face that stared back was her face—that is, the eyes were her eyes—but the hair was no longer short and curly; it was piled high atop her head in a great golden-red pompadour. An ecru, pin-tucked blouse with a standup collar circling her neck with lace had replaced her simple sweater. Quickly, she glanced down at herself afraid of what she would find, but no, her beige sweater and skirt were still there. She touched them, rubbing the material with her fingers, feeling the familiar texture. Hesitantly, she gazed back toward the mirror. The vision, pompadour and all, remained, peering out with frightened eyes as Kristen moved back to get a full-length view. The blouse was tucked into a narrow-waisted, floor-length skirt. Suddenly a man's face appeared behind the left shoulder of this image in the mirror. He had a rugged, not-quite-handsome, roguish appearance with auburn hair, a beard and mustache, and eyes that twinkled mischievously as they sought hers in the mirror.

She whirled to face him. *How dare he invade her space—her privacy—and in the bathroom of all places.* She opened her mouth to tell him off, but the room was empty and the door firmly closed. She jerked it open and looked up and down the hall. No one. She wasted no time admiring the curving staircase this time but instead clattered down it. She stopped in the huge hall, unsure which way to go. She looked in one parlor, and then another, raced past a baby grand piano inexplicably gracing the hallway, and sped toward a doorway. Before she reached it, a short round person wrapped in a blue-checkered apron filled the opening.

"Have you seen a ghost?" she chuckled, her rosy cheeks displaying a set of dimples that matched her twinkling blue eyes.

"No, of course not," Kristen answered shortly, feeling a little silly, "but some man walked in on me as I was fixing my hair in the upstairs bathroom. And he … he … well, he grinned at me."

The round person frowned, the dimples and the twinkle gone so that she no longer looked as though she were a model for Mrs. Santa Claus. Then she relaxed. "That must have been Joe," she said. "He's a handyman who helps out here sometimes, and he's supposed to check the plumbing for the washer. It's been leaking. He must have gone in the wrong room by mistake. By the way, I'm Mrs. Phipps, the housekeeper, and you must be Kristen. We've been expecting you." She extended her plump hand.

Kristen felt herself relaxing as she shook the moist, doughy fingers. "How do you do?" she said. "That Joe person must be very fast, for he disappeared completely in the blink of an eye."

"You wouldn't think he was fast if you paid by the hour," Mrs. Phipps chuckled again, the twinkle and the dimples once more a part of her countenance. "But come now, you must meet the Grandpapa. You've come down so quickly that he hasn't gone to the sitting room yet."

Kristen's nerves drew taut. She didn't feel prepared to meet the "Grandpapa." Her thoughts and energies had been focused on catching the invader, Joe. "Where is he?" she stalled. "I don't want to interrupt his breakfast."

"He's on the back sun porch with Hilda. Breakfast is long over. Come along. I'll show you."

Sun porch in this weather? thought Kristen. "Isn't it a bit chilly?" she inquired.

"Oh, it's all enclosed, but, yes, it is a little drafty, even though I have a cozy fire going in the kitchen. Mr. Lee sits there every day—rain, shine, sleet, or snow. It overlooks the pool, but you won't be able to tell that today."

"Maybe I should run back upstairs and get a cardigan," Kristen demurred, pulling back slightly.

But Mrs. Phipps would have none of it. "Come along, dear," she said. "We have several hanging on pegs in the pantry, for this is a drafty old house and we're often needing a wrap." She propelled Kristen through the kitchen, which was indeed cozy, the fireplace aglow with blazing colored flames. Kristen was trying to imagine a wrap that would adjust to fit this short, round creature; the tall, rectangular, Amazon Hilda; and her own slight frame.

Imagination gave way to reality as she was soon enveloped in a white, wool, knit poncho. Mrs. Phipps beamed satisfaction after slipping it over Kristen's head, but Kristen felt like a moth trying to emerge from a very large cocoon. How was she to remain poised and aloof looking so ridiculous? *I'll just have to pretend I'm Maggie*, she thought, for Maggie would remain serene and unflustered in any situation. Flipping her hair as if it were a sleek pageboy, she resolutely followed Mrs. Phipps onto the chilly sun porch.

"Hi, Kristen. Come meet your grandfather." Kristen turned toward Hilda's voice and saw a shrunken caricature of a man bundled in quilts reclining on a lounge chair. His face was so covered with wrinkles and crevices that it looked like a relief map with cheeks sunken into deep valleys through which ran a myriad of river and creek beds. The only signs of life were piercing dark eyes that seemed to look into Kristen's soul.

"So, you're Kristen," he said, the raspy voice seeming to resonate from deep below the quilt line. A bony arm with a claw-like hand was extended.

Both pity and repugnance were added to the long-held hostility Kristen had for this man. "How do you do, Grandfather?" she said in as haughty a voice as she could muster. Unfortunately, the image was flawed by her "Keystone Cop" effort to free her hand from the all-encompassing poncho. Flapping about wildly, she finally managed to accomplish the task.

Immediately after being released from Kristen's handshake, the bony claw pointed at Hilda and Mrs. Phipps who were watching the scene. Hilda's face showed interest, while Mrs. Phipps sentimentally wiped a tear from a baby blue eye. "Out, out," he rasped. "I need to talk to my granddaughter alone."

CHAPTER SIX

▼

"Well, what's the verdict?" Kristen was startled by the direct question and the direct look from the dark quizzical eyes.

"Ah—about what?"

"You've been examining me as though trying to make up your mind about something—my guess is whether you should hate or pity me. I'd prefer hate, if you don't mind."

Completely taken aback by this perceptiveness, Kristen hedged, "It's not a question of hate or pity. I just find it terribly difficult to understand how you could turn your back on such a fine man as my father."

It was as if she had pulled a switch. The direct look was veiled and unreadable, and the old man seemed to shrink even more into himself, if that was possible. His voice, however, was strong and cold. "I don't make a habit of explaining myself," he snapped, "especially to someone whose entire lifespan numbers less in years than the days in a month. I had hoped," he added a little less vehemently, "that we could have a serious discussion."

"Of course," Kristen responded hastily, her natural instinct to fight back curbed by her curiosity. "What is it you wanted to discuss?"

"As you can readily see, I don't have a great deal of time left here on Earth. It has become important to me to get to know my only granddaughter in the time that I have left."

"Didn't you want to get to know your only son?" Kristen burst out bitterly.

"I knew my son very well," the old man answered coldly. "That's why I knew the best way—" He broke off. "I told you I didn't need to explain my actions to you, young lady."

"Grandfather, we're getting nowhere. Just what do you want to know about me?"

The old eyes softened. "You look like her," he said. "You look like her."

"Like who, Grandfather?" Kristen was curious.

"The spitting image," he murmured. Moisture formed in the corners of his eyes, which he surreptitiously tried to wipe away. "I want to know what you're made of, whether you carry my genes or not. Can you stand up to people, girl?"

"I carry my parents' genes, not yours, and I carry them proudly," Kristen said haughtily.

"So," the old man murmured almost absentmindedly, "you dare to defy me. I guess my question is answered."

"Is it being defiant to be proud of one's parents?" Kristen couldn't seem to control her sharp tongue. "I thought it was normal to be loyal to one's family, but I can see that is a foreign idea to you."

The old man flinched, and then waved his arm imperiously. "Be gone, young woman," he said. "I'll summon you later when you have a civil tongue in your head."

"I'm not going until we finish our conversation," Kristen said boldly. "Is it my understanding that the only reason you sent for me was to become acquainted with me? If so, now that we've met, I may as well get in my car and return home. I don't think either of us is too impressed with the other."

Her grandfather stared at her. "I guess you could do that, though it wouldn't be an easy task. By the look of things, we're snowed in here." He waved toward the windows through which the unending white mounds could be seen. Kristen wasn't sure, but his eyes might have twinkled. She stood there, uncertain what to do next.

Luckily, her grandfather continued. "You're completely wrong about one thing. I'm quite impressed by you. However, one must remember there are both good and bad impressions. Which do you think that you make?"

Kristen stared back. "Probably the same kind you make on me," she said.

The old man laughed. "We're two of a kind, my girl. You had better stick around a while. Getting acquainted takes a bit of time, and even if you don't learn a lot about me, I think you'll learn a lot about yourself."

Kristen attempted a haughty, hands-on-hips, about-face maneuver, but the huge poncho swirled and twisted sideways so her arms were nowhere near the armholes, and the long fringes wrapped around her body like a strait jacket. As she attempted to free herself, she heard the old man's cackle. When she accomplished her turn, she continued out the door, hoping she didn't look as ridiculous as she felt. The continuing cackles made her doubt it.

As soon as she was out of sight of her grandfather, she shook herself like a dog after a bath in an effort to extricate herself from the wrap. Whirling across the floor, the fringe flying loose once more and yards of material billowing around her, she triumphantly did a pirouette and lifted the poncho over her head "Let freedom ring," she giggled, "I'm finally free from poncho tyranny." Mrs. Phipps and Hilda looked at her in amazement. Kristen grabbed Hilda to spin her around with her, but the move was doomed to failure. Not only did Hilda resemble a refrigerator, she moved like one too. This made Kristen giggle even more. "We're not freewheeling," she said. "More likely, we'll be free-falling. Therefore, I'm going to use my free will and some of this freedom and explore this winter wonderland. But not in this poncho," she quickly added.

Mrs. Phipps had Kristen's own coat and boots warm and dry by the fire. Kristin donned them and with scarves and mittens donated by her two guardian angels, she ventured out. The snow had started again and waist-high drifts made the going difficult. Kristen had a destination in mind, though, and she doggedly trudged the thirty or forty feet required to reach a large white mound—her car. Moving enough snow to open the passenger side door took considerable effort, but she made it. *How can people live like this?* Kristen wondered. *And, how could Joe, the handyman, ever have gotten in and out? Yet, Mrs. Phipps had gotten here this morning. Would Hilda be able to go home tonight?* As these thoughts filled her mind, she opened the glove box and pulled out the rectangular package from Maggie that she had forgotten about until a short while ago. Even with gloves on her fingers were numb, but just holding the package gave her a link to Maggie that made her feel a bit warmer.

She slipped the package inside her pocket and began the arduous trip back to the house. With the thick snow falling all around her, she felt enveloped in a white cloud, disoriented and claustrophobic. She was glad she had such a short distance to go, but when she hit the drifts, progress was painfully slow. Now she wasn't wondering *how* people lived here, but *why* they lived here. She opened the back door with a sense of achievement usually not merited by a trip to one's car.

Once inside, she took off her wet clothes, retrieved her package, grabbed the dry white poncho, and began climbing the back stairs. She had an urge to climb—up, up above the smothering white cloud. She stopped at the bathroom to peer in the mirror. No man was there—only her own rather pale face with her own short, rather wet hair. She threw on the poncho and continued climbing, this time up to the widow's walk. *Could she get above the stifling feeling there?*

Snowdrifts and ice chunks made it difficult to open the door. Kristen was ready to give up, but a last minute, all-out effort caused the door to give just enough for her to squeeze through. The cold air struck her and the swirling snow felt like needles on her face. Her hope of rising above the claustrophobic white cloud was dashed. Even the blowing air did not lessen the smothering effect of the all-white shroud in which she was wrapped. If anything, the oppressive feeling intensified at this height rather than diminished. She grabbed the railing to steady herself. The wind kept changing the angle that the needles were driving into her, and she wanted to bend her body away from them. She feared she might be leaning out over the abyss.

She closed her eyes, which only made her more disoriented. What was happening? She began to panic and had to stop a scream that wanted to tear out of her throat. Tears began to trickle down her cheeks, but before they reached her chin, they were slivers of ice. Her hair and eyelashes were heaped with snow, and the white poncho blended her into the scene. She thought of the children's picture game and book, *Where's Waldo? If I were Waldo in this picture, no one would ever find me,* she thought. She had the feeling she was lost forever.

Why had she left Florida? Why was she here? She felt like loosening her claw-like grip on the rail and letting herself float away. Surely, that white stuff must be soft, like the cotton candy it resembled, even though it hurt when it struck her skin. Slowly, without really thinking, she began to loosen her fingers one by one as she leaned far out over the rail.

Suddenly, her body was jerked back so quickly that she felt her head snap. Someone had his or her arms clasped tightly around her chest. She was spun around and shoved through the partially open door in a not-too-gentle fashion. She stumbled on the narrow landing at the top of the stairs, but the arms kept her steady. She turned to look at her rough benefactor, but no one was there. She rubbed her eyes, dislodging snow from hair and lashes, but there was nothing behind her but the partially open door. She returned to it and peered out. Nothing. Nothing but swirling snow. She forced herself back out on the walk, and using her hands on the rail, she walked completely around it. No one was there. No one. Slowly, she went back inside, pulling the door closed behind her.

CHAPTER SEVEN

▼

The next day the snow had abated. Kristen peered out her window to view this northern phenomenon. Snow was piled everywhere. The limbs of trees looked as if they'd been decorated with angel hair. Even the clothesline had a snow buildup that shimmered like a garland in the morning sunlight. Trying to guess the identity of the snow-covered mounds that dotted the landscape outside her window was an interesting game. This also kept her from thinking about the strange events of yesterday—events she was determined not to confront. There was a perfectly natural explanation somewhere. Of that, she was sure. This was the reason she had not told anyone about her experience on the widow's walk. They would surely think she was mad. But no matter how she tried to convince herself to the contrary, she was sure someone had pulled her to safety. A rational person could not deal with this, for clearly no one had been there. For now, she continued to concentrate on the mindless guessing.

She had not met with her grandfather again yesterday, despite the nagging feeling that she should have. Now she was waiting for Hilda to summon her after she settled him for the morning. When the summons came, she squared her shoulders resolutely as though marching into battle, and indeed, she did march behind the Amazon nurse general right into his room. Kristen would have saluted, but he was not alone. An incredibly handsome man was sitting beside the shrunken form, talking earnestly. He stood quickly when the two entered.

"How do you do," he said smoothly. "I'm Dr. Gullo, and you must be the 'Kristen' Mr. Lee has been telling me about."

"How do you do?" Kristen said, a bit overcome by his male beauty. She stood looking from him to her grandfather, the one so young and handsome, the other so old and unappealing. No one said anything to fill the lengthening void. She tried to think of an intelligent remark but only managed a weak, "Is grandfather ill?" As soon as the words passed her lips, she realized how inane the question was. His illness was why she was here.

She gulped in embarrassment, but the doctor merely said gently, "He's feeling quite a lot better now that you're here." His dark eyes not only seemed to hint at untold depths of compassion, but she thought she detected a look of admiration for herself. Before she could be sure, however, he turned back to his patient, gripped his hand, and said, "I'll be seeing you later this week." To Kristen, he merely nodded and murmured, "Glad to have met you." He turned from the room, with Hilda fast on his heels. Kristen was once more alone with her grandfather.

"Sit beside me," he croaked. "I want to tell you something about your father."

Kristen stiffened, but said nothing.

"I was married to a fine woman, a woman my family had always wanted me to marry, a woman of substance, money of her own and all that. Together we made a life that was, for the most part, satisfactory. One major disappointment in that life was the lack of children, for which I blamed myself. I knew I lacked passion when it came to that part of the relationship." The old man stopped talking at this point, blank eyes staring as though he were far away, lost somewhere in the past.

Kristen sat uncomfortably, wishing she were somewhere else. She couldn't imagine this shell of a man as young, a husband, or in "that part of a relationship," and it was certainly nothing she cared to be hearing about.

"All this time, my business was improving," the croaking voice began again, barely above a whisper. "My little inventions were paying off in big big ways. My pharmaceutical company had branches everywhere. I had to travel more and more. Mary stayed here, but I was off to St. Louis, New York, San Francisco. Then it happened." Again, he stopped.

This time, Kristen pressed. "What happened, Grandfather?"

"I met someone," he said, "someone who knocked me off my feet, someone who lived in a different world than Mary and me. She was gay and fey and beautiful and stubborn and very much in love—" he stopped.

"With someone else," he murmured, and the agony in his eyes was more than Kristen could stand. She rose, but he gripped her wrist. "You must hear this," he said. "She was in love with a penniless actor, and her parents, friends of mine, had sent her to me, to work for one of my companies, in the hope she would forget that shallow man. She was young enough to be my daughter and a brilliant microbiologist. She enchanted me, but she only waited to hear from her no-account boyfriend. I intercepted his letters, and she began to change, day by day. Her gaiety vanished, her rosy cheeks began to pale, and listlessness set in. I showered her with gifts and attention. One day, I found her crying and I took her in my arms to comfort her. Her sweet scent and warm body overcame me. I forced myself upon her. After that, she would have nothing to do with me although, heaven knows, I'd have left your grandmother in a minute if that lass would have had me."

"Stop, Grandfather," said Kristen. "Why are you telling me this? What does it have to do with my father?"

"Your father was the result of that shameful act of mine—a daily reminder of my transgression. Once he was born, my Emmaline vanished, and Mary and I brought him up as ours. I tried to love him, Lord knows, but every time I looked into his green eyes, I saw his mother and relived my sin. Then, when he's barely mature, what did he do? Run off with a penniless dancer. Don't you see? They both did it to me—left me for a nobody."

He sank back on his pillows, exhausted, his wrinkled skin drawn across his cheekbones and laying in folds around his neck, his eyes dark and sunken.

Kristen felt no pity for him. That was reserved for her grandmother and her kind, gentle father—two innocent victims. She turned to escape, but he clasped her wrist with his left hand while his right one riffled through the contents of the drawer in the wicker stand next to his chaise. Triumphantly, he waved a faded photograph under her nose.

"Look at this," he said, watching her closely.

CHAPTER EIGHT

▼

Kristen sat alone on the blue and white Victorian sofa in one of the pretty, little sitting rooms. She couldn't stop thinking about her grandfather's triumphant cry as he shoved that photograph into her field of vision. He seemed to get enjoyment out of the visible reaction she knew she hadn't been able to hide. She took the picture from her pocket, where she'd tucked it after insisting she wanted to keep it for a while, and studied it as if it was a map. She traced her fingers around the hair of the woman her grandfather had once loved, hair pulled atop the head with little tendrils popping out in adorable disarray. She looked at the merry eyes and the freckles that spilled down the cheeks as though they had fallen out of those eyes and scattered across this very familiar face. She let her fingers continue around the Victorian collar with the exquisite lace and the pin-tucks at the bodice. This picture bore no resemblance to Kristen's father, who surely must have taken after grandfather—although one certainly could not prove it by comparing her handsome father to the cadaverous old man.

Identifying who the photo did resemble, however, took no imagination, and that was what was so perplexing. Except for the old-fashioned clothing and hairstyle, and the faded sepia coloring, the portrait could have been of Kristen. The image was, in fact, an exact duplicate of the one she had seen in the bathroom mirror the night of her arrival. *This is ridiculous*, she told herself. *It cannot be. I'm hallucinating or something.* Her head ached from trying to make sense of it all. *There has to be a reasonable explanation*, she assured herself. *I am always levelheaded and not given to flights of fancy. I must have been extremely tired and somehow, through ESP or something, picked up vibes, which I thought made me look like my grandmother. Perhaps Grandfather was dwelling on the photo, and an image of it was transported to my subconscious.* But, no, that sounded nuts. Had she read about such things? She wished Maggie were here. Maggie would make sense of it.

Kristen walked despondently over to the Victrola and opened the two doors on the front that not only covered the record-storage area but also acted as the volume control—loud when wide, medium when partially opened, and soft when completely closed. She chose a record a full foot in diameter, with the song title "Dreams of Long Ago." It had the usual record groove on one side but nothing on the other, just a completely smooth surface. The device did not intimidate her, as she had once worked in an antique store. In fact, she found comfort in the familiar routine of winding the handle, dusting the record with the velvet duster as it spun around, and then moving the arm so the needle was engaged at the edge of the record. Scratchily, the music began to play and Kristen went back to the sofa, laid her head on the arm, and closed her eyes. She could not make out the words at all, but she liked the lilt of the tenor's voice and the whole song seemed strangely familiar. She let her thoughts drift away.

Suddenly, she was tugged to her feet into the arms of the rugged rogue she'd seen in her bathroom earlier. "What are you doing?" she exclaimed. "Are you Joe?"

"Joe? And who is that my lassie?"

"Grandfather's handyman," Kristen said weakly.

The rugged fellow threw back his head and laughed. His auburn hair flipped across his forehead with the effort, and his mustache wobbled up and down with mirth. "Nay, my love, I'm no handyman, though I guess I am pretty handy in some ways. It takes a handy man to take a ship to sea and it takes a handy man to please a woman, and many the schooner, ketch, and woman have I handled handily." He let out another whoop of laughter that exploded throughout the room till Kristen could almost see the air reverberating in great undulating waves. "But, I'm here to lay claim to the only woman I ever wanted—the one woman I never had the opportunity to please—my Emmaline." His face was now soft as he looked down at her. "Why didn't you come back to me, my darling?"

Kristen felt his breath on her cheek, and his hands on her waist felt deliciously sensuous. "I—I'm not Emmaline," she stuttered. "She was my grandmother."

At this, he laughed uproariously again. "Ah yes, I'm Joe, and I suppose you're Josephine. Emmaline, you're no grandmother. I've been an actor, played all kinds of roles, but even I couldn't pretend that you are a grandmother. But come, dance with me, my sweet. I'll pretend whatever you want." At this, he twirled her around.

The music no longer was scratchy, but melodious and sweet. He held her tight against him, and she thought she felt her skirt swirling as if it were to her ankles with thick petticoats below it. She refused to look down. She was not going to lay credence to this dream she was having. Tighter and tighter he held her, and tighter and tighter she pushed herself against him. Had she no shame? Hey, if this were a dream, she might as well enjoy it. Her cheeks were hot, and she could feel that heat spreading throughout her body. He stopped dancing, pulled her face up to his, and kissed her hungrily. She kissed him right back— just as hungrily.

"Oh, Emmaline. At last, I've found you," he breathed. "This time, I'm never going to let you go."

"What is your name?" Kristen asked.

"My name is Hilda, Miss Kristen, and you have fallen fast asleep with that old record player scratching away. I took the needle off before it ran a groove right through the thing. You must have given it quite a wind."

Kristen jumped up and looked at her watch. Only a few moments had passed, yet it felt like hours. Her cheeks still felt hot, but now with embarrassment. Hastily, she turned away. "I had quite a dream, Hilda" she said.

"You must stop dreaming and come downstairs. Your grandfather has taken a turn for the worse, and he wants to see you at once."

Kristen obediently followed her downstairs and into the kitchen where Mrs. Phipps was just hanging up Dr. Gullo's coat. The doctor was looking at her with such compassion in his face that Kristen had to look away. She had been consumed by a figment of her imagination, while her grandfather might be dying, and this good, very real, human being was worrying about both her grandfather and herself. She was filled with shame. She struggled to regain her composure with little success, until the doctor came to her rescue. "I can see you've been a bit shocked by this event," he said, "but let me assure you, your grandfather has suffered many of these little episodes and, while they're serious, I'm sure he's going to be pulling through this one too. I've just seen him and given him some medication, and once it has taken effect he'll be much better."

"You've seen him already? I thought you just got here. Mrs. Phipps was hanging up your coat." Kristen knew she was babbling.

"I got the call on my car phone and was already on my way here," he explained patiently. "I went directly to see my patient—with my coat on" he added," and now the lovely Mrs. Phipps has offered me a cup of coffee and a doughnut. Let me escort you in to see your grandfather, and then I'd like to take her up on it." He looked at her so kindly as he gently took her arm that she was immediately calm.

"That was very good of you, Doctor," she said meekly, as Hilda followed the two of them out of the kitchen.

"You must call me Nick," he said, his handsome face bent down close to hers.

CHAPTER NINE

▼

The old man was lying in the downstairs bedroom turned sickroom and, if possible, looked worse than he had on the sun porch. His arms and legs, so pitifully bony, were flailing in all directions. At least he isn't paralyzed, Kristen thought. The worst part was the terrible guttural noises he was making, spaced intermittently with the readily understood, though slurred words, "Get Kristen!"

"I'm here, Grandfather," Kristen said, all hostility gone in a sudden burst of sympathy.

"Out." Grandfather pronounced the one word clearly pointing at Hilda and the doctor. Hilda immediately withdrew, but the doctor stood resolutely behind her, one hand resting on her shoulder.

"He'll soon be calmer," he said.

"Out," Grandfather reiterated.

"It's okay, Nick," Kristen said, as she noticed that the flailing was beginning to subside. "Why don't you go for that coffee?"

The handsome man held her gaze for a moment, and then quietly left the room.

Once Kristen and her grandfather were alone, however, the old man began to babble. He obviously knew what he wanted to say, but only a word here and there was recognizable. Kristen would pounce on the word. "Sum?" she asked.

There was a vigorous shake of the head and more flailing. Kristen could tell he was frustrated.

"Son?" A nod. That would be her father.

Kristen began to feel like she was playing charades as she watched her grandfather struggling with another word after another round of babble. It sounded like "fie."

"File?" she asked

No, it wasn't file.

Fry, fly, fine, and fight were each turned down, and the old man was visibly tiring. His eyelids drooped, but the eyes peering out from under them remained determined and once more he repeated, "Fie."

What else started with "fie"? "Find?" she asked.

He nodded vigorously.

"Find son," she repeated. He really was confused. "Oh, Grandfather," she said sadly, "I fear you've forgotten. Your son, my father, is dead. It's too late to find him now."

Now his eyelids sagged shut, and Kristen thought he'd dozed off. Then, they flickered open momentarily, and Kristen could see the haunted, defeated look before he fell into a heavy sleep.

Kristen sat there for a few moments, watching the rise and fall of his frail chest. When she stood up, the doctor reentered the room, and Kristen slipped out as he began checking Grandfather's blood pressure.

"Don't go too far," the doctor called softly. "I've saved a doughnut for you."

After the dark scene she'd just left, the kitchen seemed even brighter and more cheery than before. Nurse Hilda and Mrs. Phipps fussed over her as they sat her at the big round table and placed a hot mug of coffee and a chocolate-covered doughnut in front of her. Both Hilda and Mrs. Phipps would stay the night because of Grandfather's condition, and the solid presence of the two comforted Kristen. She regretted her odd behavior in reaction to that earlier dream, especially in front of these two wonderful people. She would have lost her patience with her students if they acted so silly. What in the world was getting in to her?

As she gazed at their kind faces, she tried to put her feelings into words. "I'm sorry I acted so—so—" she began, but they would let her go no further.

"Shush, shush," they murmured as if with one voice. Hilda continued, "It's all been such a shock to you, dear. You see, we are all quite used to these things, but you, poor lamb, have just come into it. Of course, it is very upsetting."

"Very upsetting," Mrs. Phipps repeated, and wiped at the corner of her eye with the hem of her apron.

"Very upsetting," said Dr. Gullo, setting his bag on the table, "but I'm here to explain everything to you and, hopefully, find a way to make you less upset and more happy—hopefully, much more happy."

This handsome man looked at her with such warmth and intimacy that the two lovable older women quickly said, "Why don't we move you two into the parlor where you'll have some privacy with your treats?"

Once again, Kristen found herself stifling a giggle as she saw in her mind the literal translation of the words "move you into the parlor." Were they going to get a high lift, a moving van, a wheelbarrow? But, of course, they merely escorted them down the hall and then withdrew, leaving Kristen once more in the beautiful, little parlor, this time sitting on the Victorian sofa beside Dr. Gullo.

He began solemnly, "These attacks—TIAs or transient ischemic attacks— are simply temporary interference with the blood supply to the brain. Generally, the person recovers within twenty-four hours with no evidence of brain or neurological damage. The problem is that another more serious stroke may follow. Therefore, I work hard at keeping your grandfather's blood pressure down and his environment as tranquil as possible. I'm afraid he's his own worst enemy. He worked himself up into one of these earlier because he wanted to see you. That's why they sent for you—with my blessing, I might add. I feared he would work himself into a full-blown CVA or stroke. Now that you're here, he'll be more contented. It's my guess that the initial excitement of seeing you has been a little much. I think he'll be more himself tomorrow, and, of course, I'll be out first thing to check on him. In the meantime, Hilda is going to stay here, and she'll get in touch with me immediately if needed. So, you see, everything is being taken care of, and you are going to be a good treatment for him."

Was this day never going to cease causing her regret? All that the good doctor told her only made her feel worse. She had probably caused this thing with her hatred of the way her father had been treated. She had let her grandfather know how she felt, and she had left him in a huff. Her red hair, and the temper that went with it, had been readily observable. Lost in her thoughts, she was surprised to feel a light touch on her cheek. "You are very beautiful, Kristen Lee," the doctor said. "I hope we are going to be very good friends." Then, he gently kissed her on the lips before leaving the room with an abrupt, "See you tomorrow."

Kristen sat on the sofa, touching her lips, which that gorgeous hunk of man had just kissed, wondering why she didn't feel more.

CHAPTER TEN

▼

Find son. What could that mean? The words had been running through Kristen's mind ever since Dr. Gullo left. She concentrated on the words to avoid thinking about two other happenings that day—two events, two men, two lips pressed against hers each time, and two entirely different reactions. She didn't want to contemplate the meaning. Therefore, she played the "*Find son*" record over and over. *It must mean something. Or was it just the mindless meandering and muttering of a confused old man?*

She was in her room. The two comfy fussbudgets were on alert downstairs to serve grandfather or her at a moment's notice. They always made her feel secure. Their kitchen and this room were the only havens where she felt entirely safe. Any room with Grandfather in it was always frightening. The Victorian parlor, the upstairs bathroom, and the widow's walk were all sites of strange surreal experiences, experiences she didn't want to dwell on, but which had left her more shaken than she wanted to admit. The rest of the house she had declared off-limits this evening, simply because it was unknown. Nothing had happened there yet, but she didn't want to tempt fate. Like Rapunzel, she sat isolated in her tower prison, but with no way to let down her hair and no way to allow the prince to rescue her. *This is ridiculous*, she told herself. *I'm not going to allow my own foolish fears to imprison me.*

She fished out her precious cell phone—the link to home, Maggie, and sanity. She had used it to keep tabs on Mom and her caregiver, and to have "girl talk" with the giver of this unique present. Leave it to Maggie, who knew Kristen's limited resources, to pre-pay a generous number of minutes, providing a way to remain in contact or to call for help in case of car trouble. She fingered the phone, but she did not dial.

Although she had discussed her grandfather's story and his puzzling request with Maggie in great detail, she had not mentioned any of the other strange happenings since her arrival. They just seemed so absurd when hearing about the normal school routine and the romantic life of a sophisticated levelheaded girl whom she admired. She couldn't bring herself to talk about: Hallucinations? Feelings? Dreams? What? Leaving out details had never been part of her relationship with Maggie, and now, although they had chattered away, she was left with the uncomfortable feeling of not being entirely straightforward—a feeling she did not like. Reluctantly, she slid the phone back into her pocket.

I guess I'll just have to face my demons, she thought, and resolutely marched into the Victorian parlor and over to the old Victrola. She opened the doors and pulled out a stack of records. Sitting on the floor, spreading the records around her, she was surprised by the selection she found. There were fliers stuck between the records from Hutchen's Music House, 118 Main Street, Lockport, dated 1924. She also pulled out catalogs, which were marked up showing that some records had been purchased from Victor Talking Machine Company and others from The Aeolian Company. A 1921 brochure listed the price as eighty-five cents. There were also Columbia records. Kristen scanned the titles ranging from "Joy of the Morning," a tenor solo by John Barnes Wells; to "Concerto in C Minor" and *Il Trovatore*; to newer records such as "Silent Night," "The Anniversary Song," and absurdly, the "Too Fat Polka." Obviously, the collection, which was large, had been accumulated over a long period of time. She wanted to believe that her lighthearted dad had been the one to add the "Too Fat Polka."

She felt a nostalgic link to her father's early life—a life she had never heard about—as she absently pulled a stack of books from the shelves in the Victrola's cabinet. The top one was titled *How To Get the Most Out of Your Victrola*. Flipping it open, she saw the inscription: "Maria Galway Lee from Henrick Lee, 1921," written in beautiful penmanship. *So her cold grandfather had gotten this for the wife for whom he had so little feelings.* It certainly must have been a luxury item back then, and the picture inside identified it as the Hepplewhite model, which certainly was upscale. The other books were more mail-order catalogs, none newer than the mid-1920s. Scraps of paper tucked in their pages listed records that the owner had dreamed of buying. *Had the novelty worn off?* Since the collection had grown, she guessed that these catalogs might have been used only in the beginning. After that, perhaps records were purchased at such places as The Phonograph Exchange in Lockport, for which she found an ad.

She began reading the Victrola book. "We are fully conscious of the wonder of the Victrola and we have learned that amid the daily round of irritating concerns and duties, we have only to turn to the Victrola to be once more in love with life and its beautiful, blessed burdens. We believe you are unaware of the extent to which the whole scale of human emotions its music may weave into the fabric of your spiritual life and your physical well-being." The stilted words made her smile. She allowed herself to think back to the music she had last heard on that Victrola. It certainly had played on her emotions, but it also was playing havoc with her mental well-being.

Dreamily, she took a record and placed it on the turntable. A few winds, and sweet music filled her ears. She closed her eyes and swayed to the music, imagining the long, ruffled skirts that swished around her ankles in that earlier dance. She longed to be able to conjure up the red- headed rogue, who had kissed her so provocatively, but he did not appear and her skirt remained stylishly short and pleated. *I guess I chased that demon right out of my life, and that's good,* she thought, still swaying with eyes closed.

"May I have this dance?" A deep male voice made her eyes fly open.

"Dr. Gullo," she gasped, feeling foolish and just a little disappointed.

CHAPTER ELEVEN

▼

"Nick," he corrected her. (It was so hard to think of him as Nick.) "I'm sorry that I startled you. I stopped by for another look at your grandfather and, hopefully, to see you, but you weren't around. I quizzed the two ladies about your whereabouts, but they felt you should not be disturbed. Hilda was leaving for the day, but since I wasn't taking their hints that I should leave, too, Mrs. Phipps volunteered to see if you would see me. She returned with the news that you were in the upstairs parlor and appeared to be absorbed in listening to music, so she did not—and I should not—disturb you. I put on my most professional face and convinced her that it was imperative I discuss your grandfather with you, Then I bounded up the stairs before she could warn you."

Kristen burst out laughing. "Only you could have gotten away with that. There must be many perks to being a medical doctor. I bet she's down there at this very moment, wringing her hands and wondering what she should do now."

"You'd lose that bet," Mrs. Phipps wheezed. The little round lady was flushed from the exertion of the climb, and her little round cheeks puffed in and out like bellows. Beads of perspiration formed on her forehead, but the smile on her face was triumphant as she thrust a huge bowl of popcorn into Kristen's hands and went over to remove the arm from the record. "Seems as though you're great at getting this Victrola going, but you always need someone else to get it stopped. You're lucky you have Hilda and me to look out for you. Don't for a moment think that we stand around wondering what to do next. Land's sake, Miss Kristen, we may be old, but we have all the experience we need to deal with the likes of you and this rapscallion. Now, Dr. Nick, I'll have no more of your shenanigans. If Miss Kristen wants to see you, you may stay. Otherwise, you're getting the old heave-ho, and in the future, young man, you will not be bounding around here unless Miss Kristen herself gives the okay." She looked expectantly at Kristen.

" I love you, you old humbug," Kristen laughed, "and, of course, I will discuss Grandfather with Dr. Gullo any time he sees fit, but I appreciate you looking out for me very much."

"If you're sure, Miss Kristen," Mrs. Phipps wagged a chubby finger at the doctor. "Don't keep her too long, young man," she said, and with that, she returned downstairs, leaving the popcorn behind.

"I really have little to report other than that I don't want you to expect a lot of improvement. There will be more of these so-called TIAs, I'm afraid, although we are treating him aggressively. The possibility of a massive stroke is always there. His heart is not strong. He is, after all, a very old man. On the other hand, he may linger on for a very long time. The main reason I wanted to talk to you is to explain …" Here, his voice trailed off.

"Explain what?" Kristen prompted.

The doctor looked down toward the floor at the toe of his shiny brown loafer, which was making a gentle circle on the carpet. He reminded Kristen of a bashful little boy, and her heart went out to him. What was he having such difficulty saying?

"What?" she asked again with an encouraging smile.

The smile did seem to give him courage. "About my previous behavior—er—about the, you know, about my taking liberties—about that—er—uh—kiss," he finally blurted. "I—I'm sorry, I had no right," he continued.

His discomfiture, so unlike his usual suave self, somehow tickled Kristen, but she didn't want to laugh. Instead, she crazily thrust the popcorn bowl toward him. "Think nothing of it," she said airily. "Have some popcorn."

His hand reached into the bowl, but the look on his face, both perplexed and relieved, was so comical that Kristen could no longer repress the laughter bubbling up inside her.

"I am used to being kissed by handsome country doctors I hardly know. It's a problem and happens to me wherever I go," she giggled. "I've been advised that to reduce the risk I need to stick to urban areas, but as you can see I can't always heed such advice."

The doctor smiled quizzically at her, not as amused as Kristen had hoped, but gallant, nonetheless. "And lucky, we all are that you came to the country," he murmured. "Please realize that although I have overstepped my boundaries,

I do find you very attractive and hope you will give me the chance to pursue a relationship at a more moderate rate."

Kristen looked at his earnest, handsome face, thinking he sounded so very much like the doctor he was. "A more moderate rate," sounded more like the cardiovascular rate he might be trying to achieve in a heart patient than of any kind of romantic patter. She searched for an appropriate response. "Let's treat this conservatively," certainly wouldn't do; nor would "As long as the prognosis is favorable." She pondered, "First, do no harm" and "Physician, heal thyself," found them both inappropriate, and then realized the silence had stretched out far too long. She quickly said, "Of course, that's okay. I think you're great, Dr. Gullo, but I hardly know you. A less aggressive treatment of this particular condition might be the best approach." She gave him an impish grin.

He smiled wanly back at her, murmuring, "Yes, yes," and took her hand.

Kristen felt an unexpected disappointment at his lack of response to her little joke—her play on words. For an instant, the memory of that raucous laughter from a phantom red-headed rogue rang in her ears. Surely, she wasn't comparing the behavior of this handsome, kind man, unfavorably with a figment of her imagination Why did she wish that he lived up to the rapscallion title Mrs. Phipps had given him just a little more?

"Well," she said, "now that that's settled, let's see if Mrs. Phipps has anything in the kitchen to wash down the popcorn."

As they made their way to the kitchen, a soft voice whispered in her ear, "The treatment was a great success, but the patient died." This was followed by the raucous laugh she had just been remembering.

CHAPTER TWELVE

▼

When Kristen went to bed that night, she could not sleep. She tripped down the drafty back stairs and helped herself to a banana and some warm milk, but her restless mind would not be calmed. She felt the two very different kisses from the two very different men. Well, they should be very different, she thought, since only one of them was real. The thought of a man from out of the past was something she couldn't begin to fathom. The garbled sounds emanating from her grandfather also ran through her mind. The one recognizable fragment, "Find son," played over and over in her head. This new world was so confusing. She had to stop thinking, and she had to get out of the kitchen before she woke Mrs. Phipps, who would fuss over her. She had to get some sleep. She started back up the stairs.

I know, she thought, I'll make a plan. Once I have a plan, I'll be able to sleep. What could she do? How could she solve this? Although the idea appalled her, the only possibility was to swallow her pride, push her loyalty to her father aside, and enter into a better relationship with her grandfather. If she could keep from aggravating him so much, perhaps he'd become less unstable, less prone to TIAs, and more coherent. Then she could find out the real reason he sent for her and choose to help him or not, as the task dictated—and finally get on with her own, more sensible life.

With this plan in her mind, she eventually drifted off into a sleep that was fitful and punctuated with half-awake dreams. Disjointed and confusing as they were, there was no doubt who was starring in them—a certain redheaded fellow who was sometimes mocking, sometimes loving, and sometimes pensive. Upon awaking in the morning, the dreams were so vivid that she half expected to find the former sea captain and actor in bed with her. What disturbed her most was how pleasant this thought was. Her body began to tingle, and she began to worry about her psychological well-being. *Maybe I should go listen to that therapeutic Victrola once more*, she thought wryly.

She was exhausted, but once up and occupied with the activities of daily living, the dreams began to fade. In their place was a vague uneasiness wrapped in a warm, sensual cocoon. As she combed her unruly locks, she knew she was hoping to see someone else in the bathroom mirror, but she remained alone. She shook her head as if to clear away such thoughts and concentrated on her plan of the night before. She was determined to stick to it and stop fantasizing about an illusory lover like a lovesick teenager.

At breakfast, when she told the two women that she wanted to see her grandfather as soon as possible, Mrs. Phipps twittered, "Of course, of course, but, my dear, you just look so tired, so pale, with dark circles under your eyes."

Hearing this, Hilda bustled over to give her medical opinion. Eyelids were pulled down, brow felt, pulse taken. "Tut, tut, your pulse is racing. You're looking peaked. I hope you're not getting the flu, Miss Kristen. You may need a bit of a tonic," she said.

"I'm fine, just fine," protested Kristen, knowing full well why her heart was beating faster. "I really must insist on seeing my grandfather right away," she said. She felt a stab of remorse upon seeing their worried countenances. "I know you're just looking out for me," she added quickly, "but truly, I'm fine."

"Of course, of course," the housekeeper began again, "but let's just wait until he's a bit more rested. He's so much sharper after he's had breakfast and been settled on the sun porch. And you, my dear, can stop gulping down your breakfast and eat at a more leisurely pace. Then, while Hilda is tending to your grandfather, you can go back upstairs and put some color on that face."

"A splendid idea," chimed in Hilda. "Those cheeks of yours could use some blush until I can concoct a tonic for you."

Kristen knew that all she had to do to bring color to those cheeks was to think back to the dreams, the kisses, her fantasy friend, but she obediently nodded to her two caretakers and followed their suggestions.

Upstairs, she ran into the bathroom to dab on some color. Once again, as she gazed into the mirror, she tried to conjure up the redheaded rascal, but, once again, all that gazed back at her was her own slightly better, made-up self. She turned toward the stairs to make her descent. Suddenly, she felt the slightest brush on the back of her neck. Was it a breeze, a loose curl, or the brush of someone's lips? She whirled around but saw no one. She stood there in the airless hall for a moment, her fingers searching for but finding no loose curls. She continued down the stairs, wondering if she was losing her mind.

CHAPTER THIRTEEN

▼

"He's ready," Hilda said, leading her to the sun porch, where the cold, chilly glassed-in area was so different from the sunny Florida rooms to which Kristen was accustomed. She felt a shiver run down her spine and a wave of homesickness overcome her.

She swallowed hard. "Good morning, Grandfather," she said.

He nodded politely at her but said nothing. He did look calmer and more clearheaded, Kristen noted. *Guess my ladies knew what they were talking about*, she thought. She sat down on a rocker near the chaise where he was reclined.

"Now, Grandfather," she began, "I want to know the real reason you asked me here." She looked him directly in the eyes and spoke slowly and distinctly, just a little louder than her normal speaking voice.

"Not deaf and not dih-dih-dim-witted," he replied. His voice held no rancor, and he only stumbled on the last word. Things were looking promising.

"And can you tell me what I'm asking?" Kristen urged him on.

He looked at her for a long moment, his cadaverous cheeks wheezing in and out like a failing bellows. He took a deep breath, then said quite clearly, "To find son—to share."

Kristen's heart sank. Back to that again. "Grandfather, your son, my father is dead."

His dark eyes pierced hers. She watched his withered arms flail, loose pale skin rising and falling in a creepy fashion. His face contorted and Kristen felt like she was watching a caricature of a horror show. "The son ... son, son, son," he got out.

"Whose?" Kristen asked, but once again, he slumped back on his pillows like a deflated balloon, only his eyes still boring into hers, somehow now more beseeching than piercing.

"See," he said, thrusting a balled-up fist in her direction. A small corner of what looked like newspaper poked out of the clenched fist. He slumped back again and began making gurgling sounds. Kristen shuddered but worked at prying the scrap of paper from her grandfather's contracted hand without ripping it or tearing his fragile skin. Once she had the tattered shreds, she slipped them in her pocket, arranged a comforter over her grandfather's skeletal frame, and eased his head into a more natural position, which reduced the guttural sounds but did not eliminate them.

She quietly left the room to look at the paper scrap in her pocket, but this, of course, was impossible. She was not alone. She had to deal with the kindnesses of Mrs. Phipps. Resigning herself to the inevitable, she began trying to pump the dear soul about her grandfather's morning activities, hoping to ascertain how he had come to be holding that paper scrap. Her efforts were in vain.

"My dear, you'll just have to talk to Hilda about that. She's the one who takes care of him. I'm just the little old housekeeper—destined to stay in this little old kitchen and take care of the likes of you."

Kristen sighed. "I know, and aren't I the lucky one?" She grabbed a blueberry scone off the table and began nibbling. "Where is Hilda?" she asked.

"Oh, she's up in the attic. Let me get you some clotted cream for that scone and a nice cup of tea." She bustled off, and then returned with the goodies before Kristen could protest.

"This is delicious," Kristen said, munching and sipping away. "What's Hilda doing in the attic?"

"I can't say, my dear. Like I say, I'm just the little old housekeeper. She has her job, and I have mine. Now, when it comes to you, we're so glad we both have you." Blue eyes twinkled.

"Well, then I really am lucky," Kristen said, giving the rotund little figure a hug. She didn't believe that the housekeeper knew so little about the goings on in this household, but whatever she might not be sharing, Kristen knew it was completely guileless. "I'm going to hunt up Nurse Hilda and snoop into her job, just like I snoop into yours."

With that, she ran up the stairs and into her room, where she closed and locked the door. She couldn't wait to see what her grandfather had given her. She sat down at the desk and with trembling hands, pulled the badly mutilated paper from her pocket.

She was staring blankly at an obituary notice. It was for a Patrick Corral, who had died at age seventy-nine and was survived by one daughter, Livia Corral Brady, and one grandson, Patrick Corral Brady. It mentioned that he had been a captain for the Great Lakes Shipping Company, and had acted in a number of plays at the Star Playhouse in Buffalo, New York. There was a creased, partially torn photo, faded with time. Still, Kristen recognized it immediately. Her phantom had surely been a real live human at one time. Kristen forgot all about Hilda and the attic as she sat alone staring at the clipping and wondering why there had been no mention of his wife.

CHAPTER FOURTEEN

▼

Nick Gullo was downstairs when Kristen raced into the kitchen

"Where are you going so fast?" Mrs. Phipps asked, looking a bit flustered by the abruptness of Kristen's entry.

"I have to go to the library," Kristen called over her shoulder, grabbing her coat off the peg by the door.

"I'll take you." The doctor jumped up.

"Put on your boots, young lady," Mrs. Phipps called sternly.

Kristen dashed out the door, boots in hand, the doctor at her heels, leaving Mrs. Phipps wringing her hands in the doorway.

"My car," Nick panted. Kristen usually would have resented his take-charge attitude, but today she was only too happy to have someone drive her, since she didn't know where the library was or how to get there. As she swerved to change direction from her car to his, her smooth-soled shoes slipped on the ice and she sprawled in the snow. The boots flew from her hands landing directly in front of Nick who, of course tripped over them and fell spread-eagled in the snow behind her. Sitting up, Kristen burst out laughing, but she cut it short when she saw Nick's face. Losing his dignity was not that humorous to him. She bobbed up, dusted herself off, and extended a hand to him.

The ride to the library was quiet. Once there, with Nick leafing through a *Time* magazine, Kristen enlisted the help of a librarian and was soon looking at the same obituary notice on microfiche. The photograph of Patrick Corral looked exactly like the rogue of her dreams. So, whom had she been dancing with? She kept reading through the short notice, but there was little to glean from it. Just as she first read it, she was struck by the fact that there was no mention of his wife. Her grandfather had said "the son." Did he mean Emmaline's son? Had she eventually married Patrick? Had she preceded him in death? Had Patrick been married to her grandfather's obsession? If so, what had happened to her? Slowly Kristen made her way back to Nick. She knew what she must do. She had to find a way to get in touch with Patrick's progeny, although she could not imagine why her grandfather wanted her to find him since he had hated the father so much.

On the way home in the car, she decided to question Nick. After all, he had a busy practice in Lockport and would know a great many people—maybe not personally, but at least by name. "Do you know anyone named Corral who lives around here?" she asked

"Several," he answered, looking at her curiously.

"Anyone named Patrick?" she asked eagerly.

"Can't say that I do. I think I'd remember that name. Why do you ask?"

"What about a Valdez or a Brady?" Kristen rushed on, ignoring his question.

"No. I have a Kirk Valdez, a Carol, and an elderly man named Pete Brady as patients. I could ask them if they know of anyone by those names."

"Oh, please do. I also could go through the phone book. I have a little laptop but no Internet access from Grandfather's. Otherwise I could do a search on that."

"Looking up an old boyfriend?" he asked, a little stiffly.

"No, nothing like that," Kristen answered, thinking it was more like collecting data on a new fantasy one. "I'm … uh … just doing a little research for Grandfather."

They pulled into the driveway. He turned toward her as he removed the key from the ignition. "I'm very glad to hear that," he said. "As I've mentioned before, I'd like us to get to know each other a lot better. You're a beautiful girl." He reached out his arm as if to draw her closer.

Kristen opened her door and hopped out, pretending not to notice his move. "I'm sure we're going to be great friends," she said, smiling. "In fact, I think we're great friends already."

He followed her toward the house, a slight smile on his lips, but hurt in his eyes. "You're welcome to use your laptop or the computer in my office anytime," was all he said.

Why, oh, why did she always foul things up? If she had known when she left home that a handsome well-off doctor was going to fall for her, she'd have been delighted. Now, she just couldn't get that excited. Something must be wrong with her.

Just then, an upstairs lace curtain moved and she spotted a handsome face with a shock of red hair peeking out. Her heart pounded, her body trembled with excitement, passion, or something she couldn't define. She broke into a run, racing into the house and up the front stairs. As she rounded the curve, she saw him standing at the top by the newel post. She threw herself into his arms. "There, there, Lassie," he said. "You belong to me. We both know you belong to me." He began kissing her eyes that were welling with tears, and then moved to her lips. She answered him back, salty kiss for salty kiss.

"I don't care who you are," she whispered. "I *want* to belong to you." With arms twined around him and eyes tightly closed, she held on for dear life.

"Miss Kristen, are you okay?" Nick was standing two stairs below her with a curious look on his face. "Why are you clinging to that newel post?" he asked.

CHAPTER FIFTEEN

▼

Kristen was still shaken the next morning. She kept replaying yesterday in her mind. There had been no sign of the man she had told she wanted to belong to after she opened her eyes. With both arms twisted around the stair rail, tear-stained cheeks, and what must have been a completely foolish look on her face, she had been embarrassed beyond belief. What in the world was wrong with her? Dinner had been so difficult for her—a dinner that included Nick as a guest, much to her dismay. She had to keep smiling, make small talk, and avoid the strange looks he was giving her. The overwhelming embarrassment she had been feeling was eventually replaced by anger. She knew she had no right to get mad, but what right did he have to be following her, anyhow? This was her grandfather's house. She deserved privacy here. Anger gave her something to focus on other than her own ludicrous behavior. Once the meal was over, she excused herself stiffly and stalked up to her room—this time leaving behind not only a hurt look on Nick's face, but one on Mrs. Phipps' usually sunny countenance as well.

This morning, she was remorseful. Not only was she a hallucinating mental case, but she was turning into someone she didn't like as well. She needed Maggie. Maggie, however, would be in class. She would have no chance to talk to her until after school. She wandered from room to room, and then spent some time reading to her grandfather. Nick was conspicuous by his absence, so there was no way to make amends with him. She did hug Mrs. Phipps and try to explain away her previous night's rudeness as extreme fatigue. The ever-kind Mrs. Phipps patted her shoulder, but Kristen was unsure if she had accomplished her mission.

By the time lunch was over, Kristen was disgusted with herself and determined she was not going to waste the afternoon in the same lethargic manner. She decided to take a walk and rushed upstairs and then into the bathroom to change into jeans. As she tugged on the zipper, she knew Mrs. Phipps's scones had taken their toll. The zipper would not budge. No worry. Kristen knew what to do. She lay down on the bathroom floor and fumbled for the zipper, but somehow her fingers could not find it. Puffing, she lifted her head, but it was not the zipper she spotted, rather high-buttoned shoes peeking out below bloomers and a hiked-up long skirt. The worst part was that her redheaded friend was standing by her feet, his head thrown back, roaring with laughter. "My lady, my lady," he said. "You are so funny. You have changed from the modest serious lass I knew into this enchanting minx rolling around on the floor. Are you trying to impress me, my dear? No need of that. I like you just the way you are."

"It—it was the scones, or maybe the doughnuts," Kristen began to babble, putting her hands on her hot cheeks and over her eyes. Why was she so embarrassed to have this man see her bloomers? She was a Florida girl who wore shorts and minis and bikinis, which were certainly more revealing than these lacy pantaloons. She took her hands off her eyes to pull her skirt down, but she found herself alone lying on the floor with unzipped jeans. Quickly she zipped them, jumped up, and raced into the hall looking for the rascal, but as was becoming routine, he was nowhere to be seen.

I think I need a doctor, she thought, *but not Nick, no, definitely, not Nick. I need a psychiatrist. I will discuss this with Maggie when I talk to her. Now I will put this out of my mind and go for my walk.* She stuck her stubborn little chin in the air, grabbed her wraps, and marched downstairs and out into the afternoon sun. She could smell spring in the air. The snow and ice of yesterday were melting into ugly, muddy puddles, but the sun and the faint twittering of birds gave her the promise of better times to come, along with an aching homesickness for the Sunshine State. The North was teaching her that the world could look beautiful all white and glistening one day, change into ugly drabness the next, and still give the hint of better days ahead. *I need to look at life in the same way,* she thought. White and beautiful brings the discomforts of cold and damp; sunny and beautiful brings the discomforts of hot and sweaty. Life always has discomforts and bad parts, but the sun is always waiting to peek through.

She trotted off, feeling much better. She saw some squirrels and they made her laugh as they scampered around, cocking their heads at her and chattering. Her body felt invigorated. Her soul felt invigorated. She walked, she skipped, she ran, and breathed in the aromas of this new world. After an hour, she headed back toward the house, a new person. She opened the back door in a happy mood. Then, it hit her. She was still Kristen, a person who was seeing things that weren't there.

CHAPTER SIXTEEN

▼

The next afternoon, Kristen called Maggie, determined to get a hold on reality.

"You must come here during spring break," she begged. "I really, really need you. I have so much to talk to you about."

"Of course, I'll come. I'm dying to see you and meet all the new folks in your life," Maggie said.

The two chattered away, catching up on many things, but Kristen never mentioned the main reason she so needed the steadying common sense of Maggie. Her encounters with the sea captain and actor remained Kristen's guilty secret, and her conscience nagged at her because of this deception. Her relationship with Maggie had always been one of complete honesty, and although she hadn't lied per se, she had lied by omission. She hung up with Maggie telling her she would call when her travel plans had been made.

Kristen felt both delighted and worried following the phone call. It dawned on her that this was not her home, yet she had invited a guest without anyone's permission. Whom should she ask? It was grandfather's house, yet he was in no condition to make decisions, even if she could make him understand. His health had been deteriorating daily. The housekeeper or nurse did not have that authority. The doctor certainly had no say in the matter. She decided that she would ask Hilda if she thought it would be too much to consult her grandfather.

Hilda looked surprised when Kristen finally tracked her down. She was wiping everything in Grandfather's bedroom with some type of antiseptic. "I do this every morning while he's in the sunroom," she explained.

"But, he doesn't have an infection, does he?" Kristen asked.

"No, no, but you can't be too careful. I certainly don't want him to get one on my watch," she declared "What can I do for you? You look very … well, I guess I'd say uneasy," she said, looking carefully at Kristen's face.

Kristen explained her dilemma. Hilda, who was lifting an armchair up with one burly arm and not even breaking a sweat, looked even more surprised. "Why, Miss Kristen," she said, "That's no problem. Before you came here, your grandfather told us that during your visit, you were the mistress of the house and we were to do whatever you wanted."

Kristen didn't know whether to believe this or not. Her grandfather had certainly given no indication that she had any standing when she arrived, and he was the same man who had shunned her dad for years. *Was Hilda lying? Oh my*, she thought, *Once you start being deceitful, you begin suspecting others of the same thing.*

"You run along and talk to Mrs. Phipps so she can ready things for your friend—and stop that scowling," Hilda said.

"Sorry," Kristen said. "I was thinking bad thoughts." Without further explanation, she ran down the stairs to the kitchen to confront Mrs. Phipps.

"How wonderful," Mrs. Phipps exclaimed, clapping her pudgy hands together. "Two young girls at Lakeview—this will really brighten up the place."

"Do you think Grandfather will mind?" Kristen asked.

"Of course not. He told us we were to treat you as the mistress of the house while you were here," Mrs. Phipps answered promptly. *Well, that takes care of my bad thoughts*, Kristen decided.

"We must have a party for your friend. That's what we'll do. We'll have a party. Oh, two young, happy girls in this house," she exclaimed delightedly, "so much better than one morose, mysterious lady," she finished almost under her breath.

"Do you think I'm morose and mysterious?" Kristen asked sharply.

"Oh … oh no, not you, dear." Her hands fluttered, and she tried to regain her composure. "I don't know why I said that."

No matter how Kristen tried, she could get no more from Mrs. Phipps on that subject. She only wanted to talk about The Party. What should they serve? Who should they invite? How should they decorate? Since Kristen knew no one other than those immediately involved with the household, she wasn't much help. She simply wanted to have Maggie all to herself for some good common sense talks.

She did think Maggie would enjoy a party, though, so she tried to show interest while her mind focused on what Mrs. Phipps meant by a mysterious lady. Had she also seen the lady who looked like Kristen's grandmother? Was there something in this house that affected others as well as Kristen? Did this mean that Kristen might not be losing her mind?

CHAPTER SEVENTEEN

▼

Nick and Kristen were waiting at the Buffalo airport for Maggie's plane to arrive. Kristen could hardly contain her excitement. It seemed like years since she had seen her friend. Nick was not the most pleasant companion. He was a bit out of sorts due to Kristen's indifference to his romantic overtures. This did little to dampen Kristen's high spirits. Sipping her Starbuck's chai tea latte, her eyes scanned the crowd passing security. She wished for the good old days before 9/11, when you could actually wait at the gate for passengers. She begrudged every additional minute she could not spend with her friend.

"Hello! Hello!" Suddenly, Maggie was there. She glided toward them in a soft, blue, full-length coat with white scarf and mittens and a white fur tam cocked saucily over her sleek blonde pageboy. She looked like she had lived in the frigid North her entire life, not in sunny Florida. The only problem was that today was a mild spring day in Buffalo, and Kristen and Nick were in jeans and light jackets. It didn't matter. It was Maggie who looked perfect, and drew admiring glances from every quarter. The two girls fell into each other's arms, laughing and crying and talking all at once as two close girlfriends do.

"Oh, my," Kristen said, suddenly remembering her manners. "This is Nick Gullo. He's Grandfather's doctor."

Maggie took the doctor's outstretched hand and said, "Leave it to Kristen to go off into the wilderness and find a perfectly gorgeous man." This was so completely unlike Kristen's previous life that the two of them again resorted to giggles. The doctor seemed mesmerized by Maggie and seemed oblivious to their silliness.

The ride home was much more comfortable as they became acquainted and Nick returned to his normal charming ways. Maggie kept the conversation going, expertly including both Kristen and Nick. By the time they turned into the driveway of the big house looming in the mist before them, they appeared to be three friends. When Maggie got out of the car, she stood looking up at the Victorian structure before her. "Who is that?" she asked, pointing at the widow's walk.

Nick and Kristen both looked upwards. "I don't see anyone," Kristen said, "Just mist and clouds."

"Nor do I," said Nick.

Maggie was shaking her head in bewilderment. "I swear I saw you up there, Kristen, all dressed up in a long dress. I could see your red hair clearly."

Nick laughed easily. "You're seeing Mrs. Phipps's ghost," he said, "although she's never been able to describe her. She explains her more as a sad creature always skulking around in the shadows. The townspeople all believe the house is haunted, but I've never seen or heard anything like that, and I've been coming here for years. I think the mist around the widow's walk, which takes several shapes, may well be what you've seen. Better not mention the illusion to Mrs. Phipps though, or it will add credence to the myth. I assure you, the only redhead I've seen around the place has been Miss Kristen, and her presence has made even Mrs. Phipps forget about ghosts." He smiled at Kristen.

"You never told me there were ghosts here." Kristen sounded accusing, and she tried to tone that down by smiling back.

"Well, because there aren't," he said reasonably, and a little defensively. "There are no such things as ghosts. Mrs. Phipps is a dear little woman with a vivid imagination fueled by the rumors she has heard from previous employees and visitors here. I questioned Hilda, and she has never seen or heard anything either. Between us, I think we have finally convinced the housekeeper of the truth."

I don't think you have, thought Kristen, remembering what Mrs. Phipps had said about a morose creature. She also knew that she herself had been seeing a redheaded apparition of the opposite sex occasionally. She should have been relieved that someone else was seeing things also, but somehow, she didn't want her rogue to be a ghost.

"Well, I don't want to be convinced," giggled Maggie. "What could be more fun than staying in a house with a ghost—the Mysterious Lady of Lakeview? This will be a real adventure." She grabbed Kristen and hugged her again.

And you don't know the half of it, thought Kristen. They entered the house, and Mrs. Phipps and Hilda were immediately under Maggie's spell. Kristen was dying to get Maggie to herself, but Nick showed no inclination to leave and the ladies wanted to talk. Thick sandwiches, milk, tea, cheese, and fruit accompanied this conversation. Finally, Kristen began to squirm. She tried to catch Maggie's eye, but Dr. Gullo had her attention. She began to stand, but Mrs. Phipps quickly interjected, "Sit, sit. Let's plan the party while all of you are here together."

Sighing, Kristen sat back down. Nick came up with several names to be invited from the hospital staff. Mrs. Phipps said her daughter had a new boyfriend, and she was sure they would like to come. Hilda, to Kristen's complete amazement, blushed bright red and said she had a gentleman friend who might like to come. Maggie was to be the guest of honor with all those intern friends of Nicks to entertain her. Only Kristen could think of no one to invite. They all assumed that Nick would be her special date. Even though she wasn't really interested in a romance with him, she was a bit hurt by the way he seemed to be mesmerized by Maggie. The one person she would like as her date wasn't a person at all. She closed her eyes and thought back to how she had felt in his arms, how she felt as he kissed her.

Suddenly, there was no sound in the room. She opened her eyes to see them all staring at her. "Are you all right, Miss Kristen?" Hilda asked. Kristen jerked her eyes open as waves of heat and embarrassment engulfed her.

CHAPTER EIGHTEEN

▼

"It's easy to see that you're in love with him," Maggie said later, when they were alone in the sitting room at last. Nick had gone to Lockport Memorial Hospital to check on some patients. Hilda was going to get Grandfather ready for bed after a bit and then would be heading home. Mrs. Phipps was busy making scones.

"What are you talking about?" Kristen was startled. What had she given away? She hadn't said a word.

"You're in love with the doctor. I am a little surprised. At the airport, you seemed rather indifferent to him. Downstairs though, when you thought no one was watching and you began daydreaming, it was easy to see that you were in love."

"You're wrong. You're wa-rong." Kristen was almost stuttering. She couldn't bring herself to tell the person she had always told everything to that she had been daydreaming about—about what? She couldn't even put it into words—someone who no one else ever saw? Someone who wasn't even real? At that very moment, a violent rattling at the window startled both girls.

"What was that?" Maggie ran to the window, but all seemed calm.

Only Kristen saw an angry face for a second, a face with a shock of red hair, a face that mouthed the word, "Doctor" with a scowl. She tried to gather her wits about her. "I think it was a spring gust," she said.

"Hmmm," Maggie said mildly. "In Florida, a gust like that is usually only felt during a hurricane."

"Well, it's different here," Kristen said, defensively. Just then, Mrs. Phipps entered the sitting room with a little tray of tea and warm scones with real clotted cream for "her girls."

"That was some clatter wasn't it, Mrs. Phipps?" Maggie said brightly.

Mrs. Phipps looked quizzical. "Why, it's been as quiet as a library around here, Miss Maggie. What in the world are you talking about?" Now it was Maggie's turn to look quizzical.

The window just rattled a little," Kristen said quickly.

"A little?" Maggie said indignantly. "It sounded like a freight train."

Again, Kristen tried to step in quickly. "You know how the windows in this old house sometimes make a lot of noise, Mrs. Phipps? It was probably that."

"More likely, the Lady," Mrs. Phipps muttered under her breath, so faintly that only Kristen heard her, but even Maggie noticed the tremor of her hands as she poured their tea.

"Are you on some kind of medication?" she asked the housekeeper.

"Oh, my, no, Dear," she answered quite calmly. "That pot was just a little too heavy for these little hands." With that, she abruptly left them alone again.

"What was that all about?" Maggie asked.

"They fuss over me all the time," Kristen responded, not wanting to get into anything else. "We just finished eating, and we're being served tea. It never ends. Their lives have been very dull with only Grandfather for company. They love Dr. Gullo, but his visits are sporadic. My arrival delighted them, and they spend their time figuring out new ways to fuss over me. Now that you're here, they're beside themselves. We don't need a party, but I think they do and they deserve one." She kept chattering non-stop.

Maggie looked at her. "Something's going on with you, Kristen," she said. "What is it? This is me, Maggie, your friend who shares everything with you. What gives?"

Kristen had thought that just having levelheaded Maggie around would stop her hallucinations and everything would be fine. The window episode had convinced her otherwise, as had Mrs. Phipps's mumbling. She simply could not bring herself to discuss, even with her friend, the absurd things that were happening to her. Maggie would send her to a psychiatrist or a counselor. She was saved from answering by Hilda rushing in.

"Your grandfather's had another very bad spell. He's not responding. I've called Dr. Gullo at the hospital, but it will be a while before he gets here. I think you should come down," she said apologetically, looking at Maggie.

"Of course," Kristen said at once. "Maggie will come with me. She's a nurse, you know."

They made their way to Grandfather's bedroom—a room in which Kristen had never spent much time. It was dark and oppressive. Thick, faded, velvet draperies were pulled at the windows. One tiny lamp illuminated a shrunken figure looking lost in a king-sized four-poster bed shrouded in masses of the same thick, faded velvet as the drapes. He was lying on his back with his head tilted backward and his eyes rolled up into their sockets. Terrible rattling noises were emanating from him. Hilda and Maggie immediately went to him and slid him over to the edge of the bed near a portable suction machine, which Hilda switched on and began using on the patient..

Kristen could see thick gobs of yellow mucus filling the suction container, and she felt nauseated. She stumbled backward and caught herself on the bureau. She needed air. She turned and caught a glimpse of herself in the crackled bureau mirror—only it wasn't herself. It was the lady who looked like her, with the piled up hair, the pin-tucked high-necked blouse, and the long skirt. She turned and fled.

CHAPTER NINETEEN

▼

It was a long and eventful night. Hilda refused to go home and leave her patient. Maggie checked on Kristen and banned her from the sick room saying, "I now know why you're a cosmetologist and not a nurse. You stay with Mrs. Phipps, go to bed, or read a book. I'll stay with your grandfather and Hilda and keep you informed." Mrs. Phipps, in the kitchen as always, kept the tea and coffee going and a good supply of food "to keep their strength up."

Dr. Gullo also seemed disinclined to leave for the night once he arrived. He was filled with admiration for "plucky Maggie," and this unlikely medical team worked together like a well-oiled machine, checking vital signs, administering anticoagulants, hanging IVs, suctioning, sponging, and changing linens. Occasionally, they would huddle together outside the room murmuring in low voices, and then Maggie would come to Kristen with their latest medical report.

It was all very depressing to Kristen, but she noticed that Maggie seemed to be glowing. Dr Gullo was cheerful and chatty, despite his long hours. Hilda was the usual Hilda and Mrs. Phipps her jolly self. All were concerned for Grandfather, but the atmosphere did not seem to affect their moods to the extent that it did hers. Only Kristen flinched when she heard that terrible rattle in his throat. Only Kristen's own heart seemed to stop when his labored breathing stopped for several seconds at a time. Only Kristen shrank from the sights, sounds, and smells emanating from the sickroom. And, she'd had another hallucination. What was wrong with her? Even Maggie fit in here better than she did. Maybe she did need a psychiatrist. Maybe she did need a counselor.

She didn't want to sit with Mrs. Phipps in the kitchen; nor did she want to go to bed. She knew she couldn't get interested in reading a book. She wandered up to the sitting room with the Victrola and began playing a waltz. She closed her eyes trying to conjure up her make-believe friend, but when she opened them, she was still alone. She sat down on the uncomfortable Victorian sofa and began to sob. She had never felt so alone. She had a grandfather to whom she just couldn't feel close. She loved Hilda and Mrs. Phipps, but they were just transient figures in her life and they had lives of their own. She loved her mother, but she had to be the adult in that relationship. She sensed that Nick was falling in love with Maggie and that Maggie was feeling the same. Even Hilda had a "gentleman friend." Self-pity washed over her. Then she felt herself being engulfed in a hug.

Terribly embarrassed, Kristen did not want to open her eyes. Who had found her wallowing in her own self-indulgent emotions? She couldn't face any of them. Then she was being kissed, kissed in a way that left no doubt as to who was doing the kissing.

Her redheaded hallucinatory boyfriend was scowling at her. "Do you like the doctor's kisses better?" he asked.

"No, but he's real. I'm so alone," she said.

The scowl was replaced with a merry laugh. "I'm real," he said. "I love you. I've always loved you. Here. Here is a very real ring for you to wear. When that doctor makes eyes at you, you just look at that very real ring and know that you are not alone." He slipped the ring on her thumb (the only place it would fit) and smiled. "I can't understand everything that is going on here, but I do know that you are not alone and that you're mine."

"Well, he's falling for Maggie anyhow," Kristen said, but she was talking to herself. She was all alone once again, but she didn't feel so alone now. The big, bold, gold ring with the emerald in it was making her thumb feel very cared for and warm.

CHAPTER TWENTY

▼

Kristen had fallen asleep on the blue and white sofa and was awakened in the early hours of the morning by Nick and Maggie, both looking very grave. "I'm afraid we have some bad news for you," Nick said, trying to take her hand.

In an effort to conceal the new ring, Kristen flung her arms around like a windmill, twisting her body on the slippery silk fabric of the couch until she slid to a pile on the floor at Nick's feet. Her robe slid up her thighs exposing quite a bit of Kristen, but she managed to conceal the hand with the ring in a pocket of the robe. Before she could compose herself, she caught a glimpse of her rogue standing behind Nick shaking with mirth at her ridiculous pose. She couldn't help bursting out laughing herself. With one hand in her pocket and one trying to pull down the robe, she couldn't get enough leverage to get up. There she was rolling around, laughing harder and harder.

Nick and Maggie were watching her with astonishment.

"She's not awake yet," Maggie said, trying to pull down the robe on the writhing Kristen.

"She's hysterical," Nick said, trying not to look flustered.

Kristen made a mighty effort to right herself by pushing with one arm and kicking a foot.

Whoosh— a bunny-eared slipper zoomed past Nick's head. The complete confusion on his face sent Kristen into new gales of laughter and soon even Maggie was smiling. The rogue reached down and gently pulled Kristen to her feet.

"How ... how did you do that?" Maggie gasped. "You just kind of floated onto your feet."

"It must have been spiritual intervention," Kristen tried to keep her face grave. She pushed the ring off her thumb into her pocket, removed her hand, and held it up. "Now what is the bad news you've brought me?" she asked. "Does Grandfather have to be hospitalized?"

All smiles vanished as Nick once again reached out and took her hand. "I'm afraid your grandfather's gone," he said gently. "He had a massive stroke and this time there was no way of saving him, even though I had an excellent nurse at my side." He gave a sidelong, embarrassed glance at Maggie who, amazingly, turned bright red. "The undertaker is on his way."

Kristen was stunned at the depth of her emotions. "I hardly got to know him, and now it's too late," she said. "Poor Hilda. Poor Mrs. Phipps. Do they know? How are they?" she queried.

"Yes, they know. They had no intention of going home tonight with things the way they were. They're downstairs worrying about you," Nick said.

Kristen spotted the missing slipper perched in a potted plant. *It looks like the bunny is nibbling his breakfast*, she thought and then remonstrated with herself. *Why, oh why do I have such inane thoughts*, she wondered as she grabbed the offensive slipper, put it on, and trooped downstairs with Nick and Maggie.

The reddened eyes of the two older women told the story of how they were feeling, but as usual, they immediately gave her all their concern. Kristen felt immense guilt as she thought of her earlier foolish behavior and said a little prayer of thanks that these two had not been witness to it. They were crying and hugging her and telling her everything was going to be all right. *They're probably worried about their jobs, too*, Kristen thought, *but they're working so hard to make me feel better.*

Feeling the need to appear like a rational person in a time of crisis, she decided the best thing to do was to keep them all busy. She took charge and sent Hilda to pick out her grandfather's clothing for the undertaker. She did not want to use a funeral home, and so asked Mrs. Phipps to choose the parlor he would be laid out in and to determine how it should be rearranged. She was not up to seeing her grandfather just yet, although Maggie said it was customary for family members to view the body before the undertaker came. Instead, she asked Maggie and Nick to do whatever it is that doctors and nurses do to a body before it goes to the morgue.

She decided to go into her grandfather's den, with the idea of looking for the name and number of his solicitor. She was going to try to make sure that the two loyal women who served him were cared for, no matter what. As she looked around this completely masculine room, she thought how odd it was that she had never come in here before. A huge, oak, rolltop desk dominated the space. Parked in front of it was a black leather desk chair, its seat well worn. Multi-colored folders protruded from file cubbyholes and neat stacks of paper filled chrome box towers. Oak file cabinets stood on each side of the desk. In the corner was a computer desk, complete with a computer and printer/copier/fax. She could have used her laptop right here if she had only investigated or asked someone. An electric pencil sharpener and a round bin filled with pens and nicely sharpened pencils completed the picture.

She felt as if she had stepped into an immaculate business office, completely unlike the rest of the house. *What had her grandfather needed this for?* She was ashamed that she had so little interest in him as a person that she never even tried to find out anything about him. One wall was covered with plaques and shelves of awards. She glanced at a few of them from the Lockport Chamber of Commerce, the Lockport Memorial Hospital Board of Directors (apparently given to him on retirement from the Board), and the University of Buffalo. He must have been someone important in the community, but she had been so taken with her own fantasies that she hadn't even bothered to inquire.

She just stood there staring. *Who was taking care of things now? Who paid the help? Who used this office?* She hadn't seen anyone since she'd been here. It certainly wasn't Grandfather or the doctor. Mrs. Phipps took care of the household. She ordered by phone and foodstuffs were delivered. She certainly wasn't in charge of running everything that needed taken care of here at Lakeview. Hilda only concentrated on Grandfather. It couldn't be the handyman. Someone must be managing the finances and upkeep of this place. *But who?*

Ashamed of her own dislike of and, thus, disinterest in the man who treated her father badly; she hated the fact that she had spent her time getting involved with a figment of her imagination. She began searching for the name she had come here to find.

CHAPTER TWENTY-ONE

▼

Kristen did not find the address or phone book for which she had been looking. She was about to check through the neatly stacked papers when her eyes focused on the only incongruous item in a room where even the wall decorations were completely symmetrical: a spindle by the computer with a piece of torn notebook paper sticking on it. Retrieving the paper, which was covered with stains and blots, she saw that it was addressed to a Mr. Floyd. "Our dear girl is giving a party for a friend of hers," it read. "Here is a list of the guests we are having and of the extra supplies and decorations it will require. As you know, her grandfather said she was to have anything she wanted and she has not been herself of late. This will be good for her. See you Friday on your quarterly visit. Phipps."

Well, this certainly will lead to some answers, Kristen thought. Nick, appearing in the doorway, interrupted her musing. "We couldn't find you," he said. "We've been worried. No one thought to look here since no one ever comes here but Ansel Floyd."

He couldn't help looking around the sterile room with interest, making it obvious that he had never been here before either. Quickly, he regained his professional demeanor and announced, "The undertaker's here." Kristen wanted to ask more about Mr. Floyd but realized the timing was poor. She turned and followed the doctor out of the room, still clutching the notebook paper in her hand.

The undertaker was in the kitchen, being plied with goodies by a red-eyed Mrs. Phipps. He was short and stout and jolly despite the circumstances under which he had been called. He held out his hand to Kristen and had her confirm that the viewing was to be at Lakeview. Kristen felt he disapproved of this plan, but he acquiesced readily enough. She signed some forms for him, shook hands once again and saw him out, glad indeed that the body had already been loaded without her having to witness it. When she withdrew into the kitchen, Mrs. Phipps was looking at the notebook paper Kristen had laid down when she signed the undertaker's papers.

"Of course, the party will have to be cancelled," she sighed, as tears flowed down the pudgy cheeks like raindrops sliding down apples. Kristen nodded, her heart breaking for the dear lady who had been so excited about the simple joy of a party and who instead had been hit with the cold realities of death and possibly unemployment. She started out of the room to look for Maggie, then stopped and turned back.

"Mrs. Phipps," she said, "You have already been baking and freezing for that party. You have sent out the invitations. Instead of canceling, why not drop them a note and tell them the party is off due to the death of Grandfather, but his granddaughter would dearly love to meet them at the wake to be held at Lakeview. Then we'll host the finest wake ever given in Niagara County."

Mrs. Phipps brightened, but then was downcast once again. "That wouldn't be fittin', would it, Miss Kristen.? With Mr. Lee dead and all?"

"Wakes are enduring traditions in the family stories I've been told, and often were huge parties. We will uphold the tradition," she said. Mrs. Phipps still looked doubtful. "Let me tell you a story my mother told me about when her Aunt Ephie died. The family lived in a cabin way out in the Florida wilderness and the family didn't get together often, usually just for weddings and funerals. Family and friends came miles for this funeral. Aunt Ephie was laid out in the front parlor. After the ceremony, the men carried the closed casket out and set it on a stump. Everyone had brought food. Many had brought fiddles. The parlor became a dance hall, and they ate and talked and danced all night. My mother always said it was the best wake she ever went to, and Aunt Ephie would have loved it."

"It must be a Southern thing," Mrs. Phipps said slowly, "and your grandfather was not a party man." She paused. "He did say we were to do whatever you wanted, though. I guess he'd want us to do what you said."

Kristen nodded approvingly.

"But, we are *not* setting his coffin on a stump, young lady," she said firmly, her hands on her hips. "We have plenty of parlors here."

Kristen smiled and went to find Maggie.

CHAPTER TWENTY-TWO

▼

She found Maggie in a corner of the sun porch, but it wasn't the Maggie she knew. Her Maggie was cool and sophisticated, every hair of her sleek pageboy always in place and every situation always under control. This Maggie's hair was in wild disarray, her cheeks were flushed, and her eyes glistened. She was clasped tightly in the arms of Dr. Gullo, who was whispering, "There, there. It can't be that bad. We'll work it out."

"C-c-c-c-can't" Maggie wailed, then catching sight of Kristen, jumped away from Nick.

"I don't know what's wrong," Nick said helplessly.

"Maggie, what is it?" Kristen asked, but Maggie just buried her head in her hands and said nothing. Nick and Kristen looked at her completely mystified.

After a few minutes, Maggie lifted her head, brushed her hair smooth with her hands and after a couple of gulps managed to say, "I'm sorry. I don't know what's gotten into me."

Kristen put her arms around her and said, "I'm so sorry your visit is turning out so badly, but we all knew that Grandfather could die at any time. We'll get through this, and I'm so thankful that you are here with me. Everything will be okay. Soon we'll both be back in Florida."

Maggie gave her a wan smile, but did not seem cheered by her words. Kristen led her off, after giving Nick a solicitous squeeze of the arm, a gesture that came automatically to her when she sensed anyone was troubled. "I'll talk to her," she told him. "Everything is going to be fine."

Once she got Maggie alone, she tried to find out what was bothering her to this extent. Although Maggie put on quite a show of being back in control, she was still so unlike her usual self that Kristen was baffled. Maybe Nick had offended her with his attentions.

Finally, Maggie said, "I am so tired from being up most of the night and then losing a patient and—and, well, just being in a strange place and situation—I guess I just need to lie down for a while."

"That seems like a good idea," Kristen said, wondering if Maggie had perhaps seen "the Lady" again but not daring to ask. She encouraged her friend to rest and left her in the darkened bedroom. She went into the bathroom to get some aspirin for the headache caused by all the drama. She put two tablets in her mouth, and then cupped her hands under the water faucet to get a drink to wash them down. When she straightened up, she saw the old-fashioned look-alike once more. This time, the other lady, the mysterious lady, was standing behind her. Kristen's reflection was of herself in jeans and tee shirt. Even more interesting, the male red-haired scamp, who she had become so fond of, was looking back and forth at the two of them. Kristen whirled around, and both of them were still there, the male glowering at her.

"Who are you?" he asked Kristen. "Methinks you are an imposter for my Emmaline."

"Yes, yes, I think I am," Kristen said, as the other lady began to drift away. She took the ring from her thumb and handed it to him. "I think this belongs to your Emmaline," she said sorrowfully. She couldn't bear to look in his eyes as he faded from her sight.

Bursting into tears, she turned to leave the bathroom. There stood Maggie. "Whom were you talking to? Why are you crying?" she asked.

"I wish I had been nicer to Grandfather," Kristen improvised quickly.

"That's not it," Maggie said. "You think something's going on between Nick and me. Well, I may have had a tiny crush on him, but as soon as I knew how much you cared about him, I was determined to squelch that feeling—and I have."

"Oh, Maggie, that's it, then? I knew you were keeping something from me."

"And you from me, Miss Kristen. Did you think I couldn't read the signs that you were in love? I know you too well to be fooled."

"Well, you have been fooled, Miss Maggie. I am not now, nor have I ever been, in love with Nick. I enjoyed his attention, but that was it."

Maggie looked at her in disbelief. "I know what I saw," she said stubbornly.

"Go for him," Kristen laughed. "I am so, so positive that I have no designs on Nick other than he's a handsome, nice guy. I will dance happily at your wedding."

Still dubious, but wanting to believe, Maggie looked at her intently. "You sure?"

"Never surer about anything in my life. Now go find him."

Maggie skipped out the door, forgetting completely that Kristen had been sobbing when she first saw her.

CHAPTER TWENTY-THREE

▼

Kristen lay in bed the next morning going over the events of yesterday. *I guess I was just meant to be a matchmaker,* she thought. Somehow she felt that she had reunited Emmaline, who had to be the mysterious lady of Lakeview, with her long-lost lover. Had the spirits of the two of them rattled around in this house all this time, unable to meet again until Kristen came on the scene and somehow set all the strange happenings in motion? It was all completely illogical. Then there was the spark between Nick and Maggie, which Maggie's glow last night seemed to indicate another successful match. She was happy about that, even though she felt a little forlorn losing both of these male friends (even if one of them wasn't real) to someone else. Still, when Maggie came bounding in, she could only share in her joy.

"I never thought I could be so happy," Maggie babbled. "Who would have thought this would happen? Oh, by the way, Mrs. Phipps says you need to get up, get dressed, get breakfast, and be ready to meet that solicitor today."

Kristen jumped up, grabbed a navy suit, and went into the bathroom to bathe. She hopefully checked the mirror, but there were no more hallucinatory figures, and somehow she knew there wouldn't be. She dressed in her conservative suit and followed the happy, once more perfectly coifed and fashionably dressed Maggie downstairs. She wasn't surprised to see a beaming Nick with eyes only for Maggie at the breakfast table. He'd need to hustle to make his rounds and get to his office. This must be true love. Both Hilda and Mrs. Phipps were beaming, too; they loved the romance. Once more, Kristen felt left out, but she tried to put on a happy face even though it didn't quite meet the beaming standard.

Once breakfast was over, there was a knock on the door and the solicitor was there. He was short and rotund. When Mrs. Phipps stood beside him and introduced him as Mr. Ansel Floyd, Kristen could hardly conceal a smile because they so reminded her of Tweedledum and Tweedledee. His blue eyes were shrewder than the housekeeper's, his white hair much sparser, and there were no springy curls, but they could have been brother and sister. Kristen hoped he was as kindly as his look-alike.

It was easy to see that he was familiar with the house and with Grandfather's study. Kristen was surprised when he took the chair across from Grandfather's desk rather than the chair behind it, which left her standing near the doorway wondering what she should do.

"Sit down, sit down," he said, waving her toward her Grandfather's chair. "This is where I always sat, even after your grandfather became incapacitated. It does me good to see another family member fill his seat, which has been vacant so long."

" I … I'm not a real family member. I never met him until recently," Kristen remained standing.

"You have his blood and are the only one here who does," he said, "so please be seated."

Yeah, tainted blood, Kristen thought, but she reluctantly made her way around the desk and sat down as the lawyer opened his briefcase and began laying out papers on his side of the desk.

After a very long silence, he cleared his throat and fixed those blue eyes on her, "You have inherited half of a very large estate," he said.

Kristen gasped. "I don't deserve it," she said. "I didn't really like him all that much. He and my father were estranged."

Mr. Floyd was undaunted by this revelation. "He was a hard man to get to know, and not always easy to get along with. Nevertheless, this is not about personalities. This is about the law, and this is a perfectly legal document. What you do with your share is your business, but I hasten to assure you, it is yours, whether your association with the man was close or not. This may have been his way to make up for his treatment of his son. I don't know. Although I have worked for your grandfather for years, we were not close either."

There was a silence, one of those uncomfortable pauses that begs to be filled. At least, that's how Kristen felt, so since she could think of nothing else to say, she blurted out, "Who gets the other half?" Realizing how awful that sounded, she looked down at the floor.

"That part is a bit confusing," he said. "Let me read it to you. 'As I believe I did wrong to Emmaline Valdez, and as I believe when she disappeared, she probably ran off with Patrick Corral, I request that my granddaughter find any child or grandchild from the Patrick Corral and/or Emmaline Valdez lineage. I want half of my estate to be divided between or among those children and grandchildren. In the event that my granddaughter is not able to do this, I want $10,000 to be used to find them. I need to try to atone for the problems I caused both of these individuals. While I did not like or admire Mr. Corral, I realize the magnitude of my sins. When I stand before my Maker, I need to have tried to atone in order to be forgiven.'"

"He never told me whom I was trying to find," Kristen blurted out defensively.

"He told you about this?" Mr. Floyd asked.

"Well, sort of," Kristen said, and spent the remainder of their time together explaining what he had said, her interpretation of it, and what she had found out so far.

When they finally joined the others, Kristen knew she had a helper for the search and a new friend. She also knew he was as kindly as Mrs. Phipps, and she sometimes thought she detected a twinkle in his eye, too.

CHAPTER TWENTY-FOUR

▼

The day of the wake dawned sunny and clear. The old house had been scrubbed and polished to perfection. Grandfather actually looked handsome and at peace in his satin-lined coffin in the parlor. Baskets of flowers were everywhere. Kristen stopped there and said a short prayer before continuing down the hall to the kitchen. She passed the piano, which was playing the same song to which she and her ghost had danced. She stopped and watched the keys undulating with no one there and was amazed that as long as she'd been there, she had never known it was an old-fashioned player piano.

In the kitchen, she congratulated everyone on the spotless house. As she grabbed breakfast, hugged Maggie when she came down, and checked on the plans for the day, she thought the feeling in that kitchen was anything but funereal. Everyone's cheeks were pink—Mrs. Phipps from all the baking and cleaning, Hilda's because her man was there, Maggie's when Dr. Gullo arrived, Dr. Gullo's from the spring breeze, and Kristen's because of the memories of the tune she had heard coming down the hall.

Maggie and Dr. Gullo went for a walk. Kristen helped set up the long dining room table and arrange the huge food platters, placing them in the appropriate coolers or warming ovens. Hilda completed sanitizing everything in sight, and Mrs. Phipps kept busy with endless small tasks. Joe, the handyman, picked bouquets of daffodils from the magnificent beds all around the grounds. He was short and stubby, with a weathered pockmarked face. Kristen watched him, thinking back to her first day at Lakeview. She knew now that he could never have been mistaken for her handsome ghost.

Kristen took a few of those daffodils and placed them in the casket with her grandfather, feeling a bit sad that he would not be able to view them from his sun porch perch this year. Although she had not felt close to him, a tiny tear rolled down her cheek. Immediately Hilda appeared from nowhere and, as any good nurse, instinctively seemed to know what Kristen was thinking. She whipped out a tissue, wiped Kristen's face, and pronounced, "I reckon he'll like that nosegay you've put there. He'll be able to see the whole garden with his new vantage point in the sky. Now, young lady, you need to call the minister to make sure everything is set with him."

Kristen obediently made the call, and then wandered back to the piano, which was silent at the moment. She opened it up but could not see how it operated. She made up a list of songs she would like played at the wake. She met Maggie and the doctor back from their walk, and the two girls went upstairs to change.

Deciding what to wear was difficult for Kristen. Not so for Maggie, who emerged in a black suit with black satin insets at the lapels, and a white satin blouse which tied at the neck. With her three-inch, black-patent, peep-toed shoes and her sleek blonde pageboy, she looked like she had just stepped from the pages of *Vogue*.

Kristen kept rifling through her own meager wardrobe. Maggie, as always, came to the rescue. "You need to look Victorian in this Victorian house. Wear this long black taffeta skirt of mine and this black lace blouse."

"You think this is appropriate for a funeral?" Kristen asked, although she loved the thought of skirts whirling around her ankles once again.

"You're the one that said this wasn't supposed to be a somber affair and that the wake was to take the place of your two dear ladies' party. This outfit seems perfect to me."

Kristen grabbed the clothes, gave Maggie a kiss on the cheek, and ran into the bathroom to change. She remembered her first visit to this bathroom and felt a bit lonely without that male presence that had so shocked her then. She looked into the mirror when she was dressed and saw only herself peering out. She did her best to sweep her short hair in an up do like the one of the woman in her grandfather's photograph. It wasn't perfect, but it was a pretty good replica. She wished she had a pair of high-button shoes.

When she emerged, she was surprised to hear Maggie gasp. "My gosh, you're gorgeous, girl. You always look pretty, but, tonight, you're absolutely gorgeous. You should have lived in Victorian times. Hey, where is that old ring you were wearing on your thumb and trying to hide from everyone? Where did you get it? That would look good on a ribbon around your neck."

"I—I found it here in the house and, er—uh—now I seem to have mislaid it."

"Never mind," said Maggie. "Let's make our grand entrance."

CHAPTER TWENTY-FIVE

▼

Kristen stood stiffly by the door of the parlor, greeting each visitor. The number of people who had come to pay their respects surprised her. She had thought it ludicrous when the undertaker had crammed more than a hundred chairs into the parlor and adjoining hall for the funeral, but now she was wondering if it would be enough. Whenever an introduction included one of the names Dr. Gullo had suggested as a possible heir, she searched the face pointedly for any resemblance to either the photo Grandfather had carried of Emmaline or the picture she now carried in her mind of her elusive redheaded dance partner, whom she felt sure was Patrick Corral. She found no one bearing a likeness to either. She knew this wasn't the most sensible way to conduct such a search, but at least it was a start. Locating the children or grandchildren of Emmaline and Patrick, if indeed there even were any, was now crucial to her. She felt a tap on her elbow.

"Are you ready?" the minister asked.

"Of course," Kristen murmured, although she wasn't. She did not want to give a eulogy. She had said she did not want to give a eulogy. Everyone said she must. She was the only living relative. It was her duty, but her legs did not want to go forward. Maggie appeared at her side and walked her up to the dais.

Kristen looked out over the crowd of people looking at her expectantly. She could not think of anything to say. Slowly, she began. "I did not know my grandfather before I came here. I was sure I did not like him. Since I have been here, I have learned many things about him. Some of them were good, such as his position in this community, which is attested to by the presence of all of you here today. Some of them were not so good." She heard a sharp intake of breath as if some folks could not believe what they were hearing.

"I learned many things about myself, also. My grandfather was stubborn, and I have inherited some of that stubbornness. The most important lesson I learned, however, is that emotions do strange things to people. I have learned to be a more tolerant human being because of that knowledge. I have learned that everyone does have good things and bad things about them, including me. I am glad I came here. I'm glad I got to know this man. I'm glad for what I learned from him."

She stopped there. No need to tell them that she had learned that he had behaved abominably, and that, even though he was trying to make amends posthumously, there was no way to undo a wrong that had hurt so many people.

She stepped down among a sea of approving faces. For an instant, she thought she saw her phantom lover peering in from the hall, but the lack of space and the overcrowding made him quickly disappear from view, if he'd ever been there at all.

The minister spoke. An elderly lady played the piano and hymns were sung. Prayers were said, and then Kristen took up her post once again, shaking hands with many of the mourners. The crowd dispersed and the huge house swallowed them up with no problem. Mrs. Phipps and Hilda commandeered the transformation from funeral home to party house as they prepared for the wake. The undertaker took the casket containing the last remains of her grandfather to the crematorium. Many baskets of flowers were taken to nursing homes and the rest arranged throughout the house. Dance floors were polished, the piano moved nearer, and a small area prepared for a deejay.

Kristen flitted here and there, caught up in the moment. "Where are the piano rolls?" she asked Hilda.

"Piano rolls? I don't know what you're talking about. You'd best ask Mrs. Phipps."

"Where are the piano rolls?" she asked Mrs. Phipps. "I want them to play "Dreams of Long Ago" tonight."

"Piano rolls? What are piano rolls?" Mrs. Phipps looked perplexed.

"You know, those rolls of paper with perforations in them that are pre-programmed to play certain music. I heard it playing "Dreams of Long Ago" this morning, but I can't find anyone who knows about it, and I couldn't see where the rolls fit and I don't know where the rolls are kept."

"I never heard of such a thing. You need to ask Joe, the handyman, I guess. He takes care of all the mechanical things around here." Mrs. Phipps went back to serving her guests. Before Kristen could hunt for Joe, the deejay arrived.

"Can you check this piano and see if the piano roll "Dreams of Long Ago" is in it?" she asked him. "I don't know how it works."

The fresh-faced young man looked inside the piano and pressed a key or two. "Don't know if you're pulling my leg or not, Miss, but this is not a player piano. There are no rolls in it. I have to get set up before the lady who hired me gets on my tail."

Kristen stood there astounded, but all she said was, "Well, I'm that lady." The young man blushed just as Maggie and Dr. Gullo came by.

"Things are going great," she said, holding tightly to the doctor's hand. "Can't wait for the music to start." She looked at the deejay with the flaming cheeks. "My, what did you do to him, Miss Kristen?" Both she and Kristen began to giggle.

"This young man is in charge of the music," she said, giving him a wink that said they weren't laughing at him, "and he is about to make your wish come true. I also hope he will make a wish of mine come true by playing "Dreams of Long Ago" sometime this evening."

"I'm not sure I know that tune," he said ruefully.

"Ah, but I have an old record," Kristen replied. "Even though you have newfangled equipment, I am sure you can turn it on your turntable, and even if it is scratchy, I want to hear it."

All three looked at her with puzzled expressions. Finally, the deejay said, "Of course, I will, Ma'am, whatever you wish."

"Great." Kristen hurried off to fetch it.

CHAPTER TWENTY-SIX

▼

Kristen slipped into the parlor that held the old Victrola, thankful that it wasn't occupied like the rest of the house. She retrieved the record and clasped it in her arms, thinking about the brimming vitality of the captain the evening they had danced. *How ironic,* she thought, *to think of his vitality. He hadn't actually been alive, had he?* She missed him desperately, but she felt he had been reunited with his true love. If any of this were real, and not just her overactive imagination, that was the way it must end. Still, she was feeling melancholy and just couldn't shake the feeling that she had lost a dear friend forever—and that friend wasn't Grandfather.

She delivered the record, which was older than its recipient. He held it in his hands in wonderment. "This thing is an antique," he said. "When do you want me to play it?"

"Whenever it feels appropriate," Kristen said, giving him a smile. She continued her hostess duties, going from room to room and person to person, introducing herself and trying to remember all the names she was learning. The music could be heard throughout the house, thanks to the strategic placement of speakers. She saw Maggie dancing in the arms of her new beau and tried to stifle just a twinge of jealousy. She watched the little housekeeper, bustling everywhere, replenishing refreshments, and attending to needs, real or imagined.

To all outward appearances, the wake was a grand success, but the hubbub was giving Kristen a headache. She decided to retreat upstairs and take an aspirin. She passed a couple on the stair landing who had found a cozy spot for a snuggle. This brought a smile to her face and a remembrance of when she had been in someone's arms in the same spot only to find out she was hugging the stair newel post. She did envy these real lovers.

After taking her aspirin, Kristen climbed up to the widow's walk to look out over the lake. The music was very faint, the moon was shining brightly, and a feeling of absolute peace pervaded. She closed her eyes and imagined the ghostly couple dancing, just like Maggie and Dr. Gullo. Her headache left her as quickly as any negative feelings. She turned and hurried to rejoin the downstairs throng, much more comfortable in her own skin.

She had met many people with the surname Corral, but none resembled Emmaline Valdez or her captain, and none who recognized either name when questioned about their ancestry. Still, she began enjoying the residents of this rural community. She had just turned away from an interesting conversation with some members of the Polar Bear Club—a group that swam in the lake in the middle of winter—when she heard the disc jockey announce that he was playing a special song for the Mistress of Lakeview. Kristen blushed and made her way to the newly designated dance floor to thank him.

The music began, and on the modern sound system, it was a little scratchy, but sweet and melodic. Kristen closed her eyes and swayed with the music. "May I have this dance?" a husky voice whispered in her ear. Kristen opened her eyes to see her phantom holding his hand out to her.

"What—what are you doing here?" she asked.

"Asking a pretty girl to dance," he answered.

"But—but," she began to protest.

"No buts," he said, and clasped her in his arms, whirling her around.

Kristen closed her eyes. "I'm making a fool of myself," she whispered.

"And why would that be, Miss Lee? Dancing with me does not necessarily make one a fool. At least, I don't think so."

"You know why," she hissed, thinking of how foolish she'd looked clinging to the stair rail. "When I open my eyes, I may be dancing with a broom," she continued through clenched teeth, but then she couldn't resist adding, "but why are you calling me 'Miss Lee' instead of 'My Lady'?"

"Well, I'll call you 'My Lady' if that is what you want," he drawled, "but I didn't know that was required, or protocol, or whatever. And no one has ever referred to me as a broomstick before. I'm rather substantially built."

Kristen peeked out of lowered eyelids. Yes, he was still there. Yes, his hair was still that beautiful auburn color. Yes, he was still that same roguishly handsome fellow dressed up in modern clothes. But he seemed a bit different, more refined, less outrageous. Then she remembered that he was an actor. He could probably fit in anywhere. She noticed the big gold ring on his finger with its emerald sparkling.

"I wasn't an imposter, Patrick," she said. "You just mistook me for my grandmother. Now please leave, and don't embarrass me in front of all these people."

"Patrick? How did you know my name? We have never been introduced, have we? And I swear I never knew your grandmother. I just flew in this morning."

"Stop it. Stop it. This is totally inappropriate at this time. You need to go back to … to wherever you flew in from … and I'm surprised to hear that you fly. I thought you just suddenly appeared." She knew she was spluttering, and she hated it.

He stopped dancing, gazing at her in amazement. Taking advantage of his relaxed hold, she slipped away and made her way to the den and office, a place no one would be likely to find her. What was wrong with her? She must be hallucinating again. She had to get over this obsession with whatever had happened within this house. Old memories lingered here just as the music proclaimed in "Dreams of Long Ago"—old memories that had somehow caught Kristen within them, even though they were from another era. Visions of the little webs Native Americans made, called dream catchers, entered her mind. Was she inadvertently caught up in some dream from long ago?

She sat at her grandfather's desk, her head in her hands, thinking about all that had happened. She allowed all the emotions she had tried to deny and hide to flow through her. She felt the excitement once again of his warm body tight against her. She felt the passion of his kiss. She listened to him say over and over that he would never leave her. She also replayed the vision of him disappearing with his true love, which she had to admit left her (the new Mistress of Lakeview) feeling terribly desolate and lonely. She brushed at a tiny tear sliding down her cheek.

"Whatever is wrong, My Lady?" a voice called out from the doorway.

CHAPTER TWENTY-SEVEN

▼

Startled, Kristen stared up at the man with the shock of unruly red hair, which tonight looked much shorter and more orderly than she had ever seen it. That, plus his clean-shaven face and modern dress, made him seem almost a stranger to her, but the same impish grin was there when he addressed her as My Lady and the same mischievous, but smoldering eyes captured her gaze. There could be no doubt as to his identity.

"Patrick," she said. "This has got to stop. I just can't deal with all that is happening and with you, too. You have to go away, and you have to stay away until we find Grandfather's other heir. Then, you and he can sort it out, and I will go back home and try to forget this whole crazy episode in my life."

Her ghost continued to stare at her in a good-humored sort of way.

"Well, I see you two have met." Mr. Floyd had silently entered the room. Her sanctuary was getting crowded. "I've been trying to find you, Miss Lee, to introduce you to him."

"You can see him?" Kristen blurted out. "You can actually see him? This is getting weirder and weirder."

Ansel Floyd's eyes widened in surprise. "Well, I actually haven't seen him as in—well, as in, seen him in my office or anything, but I talked to him before he flew in."

"Well, so did I," Kristen tried to explain." I mean I talked to him first but thought he was Joe, then he disappeared, then he just appeared again and again—just flew in, I guess—but no one else ever saw him but me. Are you sure you can see him?" she asked again.

The two men now gaped at her as if she'd just grown another head. "Miss Lee, this is Patrick Brady, the missing co-heir to your grandfather's estate. My office has been searching for him and, believe it or not, we found him in Florida, not too far from where you live. Mr. Brady is a successful lawyer, who formerly worked for the attorney general and is a good friend of the governor down there, Charlie Crist. With such outstanding connections, he wasn't really difficult to find." He beamed on this new Patrick with something like fatherly pride.

Feeling completely humiliated by her previous bizarre statements, Kristen tried to take in the fact that this wasn't her ghost, that this was a descendent of her ghost. She searched around for something sensible to say. "Well, I know Charlie Crist, too," she said. "He was Commissioner of Education before he was Attorney General or Governor. I am a teacher. I've been to meetings with him. I've ridden on planes with him. In fact, after he was governor, I saw him at Books-a-Million, and he looked at a space book with me. So, yes, I know Charlie Crist, too. Well, I'm not actually a friend, but, well, ah, we were always friendly."

Oh, dear, she knew she was babbling and the two men looked even more puzzled than before. She needed to say something sensible. Her gaze riveted on the redhead's ring. "Where did you get that ring?" she demanded.

"Why it was passed down from my grandfather, to my mother and then to me," he said. He talked slowly, as if he was talking to a child or to a mental patient, Kristen thought. "May I ask why you ask?" He was watching her closely now.

Finally getting herself under a bit of control, Kristen answered as nonchalantly as she could, "Oh, I just thought I had seen one like it before," she said. "I'm probably just mistaken."

"I guess it is a night for mistakes," Mr. Brady said, "for from the moment I saw you, your face seems so familiar. I wonder if I met you sometime in Florida."

"I'm sure you didn't," Kristen said firmly, because she knew if she had ever seen his face before seeing it for the first time in the upstairs mirror she would have remembered it.

Mr. Floyd looked baffled by both of them now, but quickly got everything back on track. "Let's all sit down and go over this estate business," he said. And so they did, but his two clients seemed more interested in gazing at each other than at looking over and signing his documents. When Patrick reached for the pen, his fingers accidentally touched Kristen's. A jolt of such excitement and heat ran through her body that she felt as if she'd been tasered. The look on his face indicated that he felt the same.

Once the paperwork was completed to the little attorney's satisfaction, Patrick looked at a now-blushing Kristen. "Let us finish our dance," he said.

And so they did. The rest of the group may have tired of "Dreams of Long Ago," but it was the most wonderful tune ever waltzed to by the two heirs of Lakeview Manor. Kristen felt completely at home in the real-life arms of her phantom look-alike, and this real human was enamored by the petite redheaded beauty in his arms. It was not until much later that he found out she was the spitting image of an old tintype his grandfather had kept of a lost love.

Epilogue

Fate, somehow, found a way to turn a tragic occurrence into a fairy tale ending, even if it took more than one generation to do so. How much of her relationship with Patrick Corral, Kristen told to Patrick Brady, I really cannot say. Some things are better not known. One year after the wake at Lakeview, however, another party was held there, this time to celebrate the double weddings of Nick and Maggie Gullo and Kristen and Patrick Brady. Mrs. Phipps tended to all the arrangements, with Hilda assisting. Ansel Floyd officiated at the wedding, and Joe the handyman built a beautiful arbor for the ceremony, decorated with flowers from Florida. The brides and grooms danced to a newer downloaded version of "Dreams of Long Ago." And yes, Governor Crist did attend.

Both Mrs. Phipps and Hilda now live at the mansion, keeping everything going when the heirs are in Florida and opening everything up upon their return. Kristen's mother also lives there full-time and is ably cared for by Hilda. Dr. Gullo has bought a farm nearby, and Maggie has given up teaching to be his office nurse. Kristen and Patrick are snowbirds at present, but Patrick is thinking of opening a practice in Buffalo and Kristen is thinking of filling the nursery that Hilda is planning.

Ansel explained that he had only recently learned that Emmaline left no heirs except Kristen herself. She had died (probably of heartbreak), shortly after leaving Lakeview and before she could come back for her son. Patrick Corral went into seclusion for several years but eventually married a lovely, educated lady named Darba DeWitt. They had one girl, Livia Corral Brady, who was Patrick's mother. After that, it was simple to find Patrick.

And Emmaline Valdez and Patrick Corral? They have not been heard from since. However, occasionally, when Patrick and Kristen stand on the widow's walk and look out to sea, what looks like an ancient sailing vessel (perhaps a ketch) passes by with two lovers entwined in each other's arms standing at the rail amongst the casks. Then again, it may just be a mirage.

THE END